praxis

praxis

David Gerrold

star traveler press

First Trade Paperback Edition

This is a work of fiction. Names, characters, places, and incidents, either are the product of the author's imagination or are used fictitiously. Any resemblance to actual persons, living or dead, events or locales is entirely coincidental.

ISBN: 979-8-9886342-4-9

Editor and Publisher, Justin T. O'Conor Sloane
Cover art: *Praxis* © 2024 by Bob Eggleton
Book design by F. J. Bergmann

star traveler press

an imprint of Starship Sloane Publishing Company, Inc.
Austin–Round Rock, Texas
starshipsloane.com

Table of Contents

Foreword by John Shirley   vii

Praxis   1

About the Author   169

FOREWORD

Praxis
noun, plural prax·is·es, prax·es [prak-seez].
1. *practice, as distinguished from theory; application or use, as of knowledge or skills.*
2. *convention, habit, or custom.*
3. *a set of examples for practice.*

    —Random House Dictionary

How do we usually dramatize interstellar space colonization? The usual thing comes down to: a spacecraft lands, the colonists check the breathability of the air, step out with weapons in hand, and maybe it seems Eden-like at first, and then shows us its hidden dangers, or maybe it's hostile right off. Either way, we're tossed in like a baby into a swimming pool. We too often skip blithely over what would be the *reality of preparation* for another world. In muscular first-person prose, David Gerrold turns this convention on its head.

Are we surprised at his bold approach? Not if we know David Gerrold's work. In his acclaimed novel *When HARLIE Was One*, Gerrold abandons the cliches about robotics and artificial intelligences, and uses it instead as an exploration of coming of age, of psychological growth and what it means to be human. Theodore Sturgeon said the novel "carries a good freight of social and psychological insight"—and that can certainly be said about *Praxis*.

Gerrold's novel *The Man Who Folded Himself* is another fresh approach to a genre convention—he has a time-traveler meet himself, repeatedly, in various timelines, and among other things he has sex with himself. Because, why not?

Gerrold wanted to boldly go where no television show had gone before, when he got Gene Roddenberry to promise a *Star Trek* episode with gay characters. A proudly gay man, Gerrold was a pioneer in this effort at bringing Gay Liberation to the mainstream. But Roddenberry was unable to get the story approved, and the episode never happened. Still—Gerrold came close. And now gay and trans and non-binary characters are standard in television, as exemplified by *Star Trek: Discovery*. The theme is enmeshed in Praxis, as our ostensibly hetero protagonist finds himself married to a gay man in order to increase the chance of approval for emigration to this rugged, mysterious exo-planet populated by male colonists only. He grows to know his husband, José, with a deep and special kind of intimacy.

Why is the planet Praxis monosexual? Because cumbersome complications arose when hetero couples had children on other colonized planets. Here again Gerrold is thinking through what is usually unexplored, in this case the social and grittily practical issues arising from interplanetary colonization.

In *Praxis*, the protagonist's transportation to other worlds isn't spacecraft, it's "portals," and he thinks them through as well:

> Opening a hole in space is tricky. First you get a bunch of scientists and engineers to design a set of probability matrices, you use these matrices to shape a hyperstate whorl, you wait until it stabilizes, and then you stick a probe through to see what you had. Of course, you put the whole thing inside a massive pressure dome, just in case—because nine times out of ten, you get a dry hole. A wall of rock. Empty space. Crushing gravity. A gas giant. Even de Sitter space, whatever that is. Once even,

the interior of a star—that blew a hole in Montana bigger than the Barringer meteor crater.

Which brings up another important aspect of *Praxis*—it does not stint on science-fiction vision. The sense of wonder is strong in this one. Gerrold extrapolates our current social tendencies into an all-too-believable future in which most people, in a grievously environmentally damaged and overpopulated world, are trapped in a form of indentured servitude. A stifling bureaucracy offers few choices to the under-privileged. Volunteering for colonization is the only way out.

Gerrold previews the peculiar judicial system of such a society and gives us a wry glimpse of the transhumanist bizarrity we're headed for now. He asks important questions our real-life giddy transhumanists aren't asking. Could over-specialization through bioengineering and cyborgian enhancement end up weakening us, ironically removing choices, narrowing rather than expanding our options?

But at its core *Praxis* is about a different kind of transformation—how an ordinary, reasonably bright human being can prepare inwardly for the gargantuan challenges of a xenobiological world. This self-transformation calls for self-knowledge at its most rigorous. In Praxis, Gerrold acknowledges that our greatest challenge is ourselves. It's a challenge we cannot meet without seeing ourselves as we really are:

> He delivered his questions in a deceptively soft voice, but his words sliced like a scalpel. "What are you discovering about yourself? Is that who you want to be? What are you willing to give up? Who are you committed to being? What support are you willing to accept? Don't sell me another plate of the

> same old bullshit that you used to scrape by out there. This isn't out there—and we don't eat bullshit on Praxis! I want to hear the stuff you're *not* saying. The stuff you'd rather die than speak aloud. Because until you drag that shit up and acknowledge it and own it, it's going to own you.

So the exploration of outer space, in Gerrold's novel, first requires an exploration of inner space.

Is the journey he takes us on without its (possibly) controversial elements? Hell no!

We're talking about David Gerrold here....

—John Shirley

ONE

It wasn't a riot. It was a celebration. Our team won. They won the big one. It was important. It was the first time in living memory that the team came home with the flags, the trophies, the rings. So of course we hit the streets.

It's traditional to celebrate. Get drunk. Smoke dope. But this was special beyond special. It was time to get fucked up and go wild. Break a few windows, start some fires, flip a couple police cars. That's not a riot. That's a party. We earned it. We deserved it. We're the champions. Boo-yah!

In the morning, the lawyers explained it to me. There were two of them. They wore shiny suits and hard expressions. The law didn't see it the same way I did. According to the law, it was a riot and I'm a bad person.

So they gave me a choice. The same choice they give everyone. Pay a large fine. Very large. Or else join the Labor Corps. Three to five years, depending on the assignment. That's not really much of a choice, but it isn't supposed to be. The law sets the fine by your projected income (and in my case, that's somewhere on the south side of nothing) but even if you have an income, the fine is always going to be more than you can afford. The judge has no incentive to make it easy on you. Not while the state can show a profit on your conviction.

The Labor Corps is supposed to be a way to repay your debt to society, but it's really a for-profit arrangement. The Labor Corps buys criminal indentures from the state. That makes it government-sanctioned slavery.

I'm not stupid; slavery is about economics. If labor is cheap enough, you can build pyramids. The Labor Corps builds pyramids—or anything else anyone has the money to pay for. There was a lot of talk about it in the lockup. There's nothing else to do in there but talk. Or sleep. Or masturbate. Alone or with a friend.

The courts are backed up like a cheap toilet, so they arraign prisoners on a first-come, first-served schedule. If it's a party weekend, you can be in lockup till Wednesday or Thursday.

Somewhere in there, you get ten minutes with the lawyers. They're not there to defend you. They're there to explain why you're going to the Labor Corps. You have no choice, they say, make it easy on yourself, plead no-contest and you'll get three years instead of seven. As soon as you realize you have no choice, you agree and they send you back to lockup to wait for sentencing.

In lockup you hear the rest of it. There are no three-year or seven-year sentences. The Labor Corps pays your fine and owns your indenture. They put you to work, whatever you can do—they don't mistreat you, but they do bill you for your bed and your laundry and your meals. They bill you for cigarettes and candy bars and jumpsuits and shoes and underwear and sick calls.

So it works out that you never quite pay off your bill. The Labor Corps isn't an indenture, it's a lifetime career.

Except maybe not.

There was a big Black guy sitting against the wall, looking hard and skeptical. I didn't know what he was in lockup for, but he had a wristband like the rest of us, blinking red and flashing text and numbers. His name was Mickey, but everybody called him Big Mick.

Big Mick was saying to someone, "Nah. Don't have to indenture. Request emigration."

"To where?"

"Anywhere. Go through a portal."

"A portal? Yeah, right. The other side of nowhere."

"Portals buy indentures, thirty cents on the dollar. Cheapest way out. You go, you only pay back the thirty."

"To where? Nordhel? Heavy-gee ice-world? Chip blocks off glaciers so Midwest farmers can water their beans? Then we get to buy the beans? Or maybe ammonia mining on some nameless rock—live inna tunnel where everything smells like piss? Work inna pressure suit, eat soylent and shit green? Uh-uh." That was a big guy, covered with a red tiger-tat, outlining the left half of his face. "Rather be digging new Sahara canal. Not hafta pay for my own oxy."

Big Mick shrugged. "Your choice, gospodin. Some people want other."

"Yeah? Name six."

"Just one. Praxis."

"Never heard."

"Private-financed. Six dry holes, lucky on the seventh. Yellow star. Point nine gee. Oxygen-rich. Post-Jurassic. Can't get better."

"It so good, whyn't you go?"

"Not taking everybody. Need specific skills. But I'm apped and good to go. Just waiting. Two-three days, I'm outa."

"Yeah? Maybe. What they need?"

"Carpenters, plumbers, electricians, engineers, geologists, farmers, dishwashers, trashmen—anybody who wanna work. Building a colony from ground up."

Tiger-tat wasn't impressed. "Issa catch. Always a catch."

Mick said, "Maybe. But still sound good to me. Planet has loopyh orbit. Go from inner rim of Goldilocks zone to outer edge, maybe past, but life survive. When hot, is too hot. When cold, is too cold. But not impossible. Least that what they say. It have one big continent, one big ocean. Lotsa islands. Thirty-six axial tilt—so hot at equator it have scorch belt across middle of continent. Uninhabitable. But north and south, issa useful climate. Poles are temperate, some good ice, but not enough meltwater for whole continent, so large areas of scrub and desert. Not paradise, but possibilities."

"But it has shirtsleeve zones, right?" asked a smaller man.

"Two," said Big Mick. "North and south. But two very different ecologies because of separation. Some big animals. Watch where you step, you be okay."

"Not sound too bad," said the smaller man.

"No listen anymore," snapped Tiger-tat. "Dissa recruiter!" He jabbed a finger at Big Mick. "You think we stupid? How much a bounty you get for us?"

Big Mick didn't blink. "If you no wanna go, don't go. Nobody hold gun to your head."

"Bullpiss. Not even good enough to be shit. No recruiter inna jail unless portal open onna bad place. Fukka dis." Tiger-tat shook his head and crossed to the bench on the opposite wall. Two men got out of his way and he parked himself there, folding his arms and glowering defiance.

A gospodin with shaved head, no tats, stepped up next. "What else? What you not saying?"

Big Mick smiled. "No women."

Shaved-Head frowned. "No women?"

Mick nodded. "Just robos."

"Why so?"

"Population control. Stability. They say."

Shaved-Head snorted and walked away. So did several others. But a few remained and continued questioning. I sat on the corner nearby, not facing, but I could hear the conversations clearly. I kept my eyes shut and pretended to doze. Safest way to wait.

Big Mick explained what would happen at arraignment. The judge would have your plea deal in front of him, but for the record he still had to ask, "Will you pay your fine or will you accept service in the Labor Corps?" At that point, you had the right to say, "Your Honor, I request the opportunity to apply for labor emigration. I request Praxis." (Or any other portal.)

The judge would then forward your resume, your work experience, and your rap sheet, to the requested Portal Authority. Or, if you had no planet in mind, you would be put up for bid. Some portals had representatives in court who could make an immediate decision on your application. After that, any other portal agent had ten days to put in a bid. If there were no bids, you went to the Labor Corps.

If Praxis had gone to the trouble of putting a recruiter in the lockup, they would probably have a representative in court. I listened to the whole discussion. I didn't know if Big Mick was a recruiter, but he did make a good case.

The suits had made it clear that I was going away. The videos of the riot showed me stark naked, standing on the roof of a police car, drinking beer and urinating on it. Despite the animal mask I was wearing, the barcode tattoo on my butt still gave me away. That and my federal microchip.

I knew a little bit about the portals. It was hard not to. Living in a stinkhole, you dream of escape, and the portals looked like magical doorways, so there were a lot of stories floating around about what was really out there. Supposedly, the best worlds were saved for the rich, where secret pleasure domes dotted paradise landscapes, but all the rest were hellish worlds where monsters and demons sucked away your soul. Zombie-rumors staggered round the webs, refusing to die, no matter how much snopery was applied.

The truth about the portals was probably much more mundane.

Opening a hole in space is tricky. First you get a bunch of scientists and engineers to design a set of probability matrices, you use these matrices to shape a hyperstate whorl, you wait until it stabilizes, and then you stick a probe through to see what you had. Of course, you put the whole thing inside a massive pressure dome, just in case—because nine times out of ten, you get a dry hole. A wall of rock. Empty space. Crushing gravity. A gas giant. Even de Sitter space, whatever that is. Once even, the interior of a star—that blew a hole in Montana bigger than the Barringer meteor crater. That's why portals are now staged offworld. You have to go through a staging world, sometimes two or three, to get to the portal that opens to your final destination.

Most of the portal worlds—when you do get one that's useful—are barren, but they're still good for mining gas and minerals and sometimes even ice. Frozen water is best, you can ship it or pipe it and there are no shortages of buyers, clean water is the most essential component of survival. A lot of gases are valuable, especially ammonia and nitrogen, because you can make fertilizer with them. Rare earths of all kinds, of course—sulfur, nickel, molybdenum, tin, all the metals. It's easier to carve up a barren world where there aren't any greenies to protest, so lots of big corporations have funded portal development. Cheap and easy resources were a magnet for poor nations too. It should have been a gold rush.

Only it wasn't. Because every useful portal had its own set of impossible challenges. The initial investment to develop a self-sufficient colony could be prohibitive. Every new world required its own specific sets of equipment and life-support modules.

But shirtsleeve worlds were always one-way tickets.

If there was liquid water, life was inevitable. If you opened a portal and you found oxygen in the atmosphere, it was both good news and bad. Oxygen meant there were plants producing it. And if there were plants and oxygen, then there were creatures breathing that oxygen and feeding on those plants and excreting waste for the plants to feed on. And if there were things that ate the plants, then there were very likely a lot of other things that preyed on those things that ate the plants. Mostly microbes and things on that scale. Usually infectious things. Where life was possible, it was inevitable—in a large messy web of complex interrelationships. A taxonomist's wet dream. A colonist's nightmare.

Because that's what Big Mick wasn't saying. A shirtsleeve world existed in a self-imposed quarantine. You could go, but you couldn't come back. Ever.

No Portal Authority was going to take the risk that something might come back to infect the homeworld. Anything shipped in from a barren world could be certified as clean—but a world with its own ecology, even a simple and primitive ecology, could still contain deadly biological time-bombs. Quarantine was the easiest solution.

And that was why Praxis needed to recruit so aggressively. It was a door of no return. If you emigrated, you could have a long life or a short life, there was no guarantee—but either way, you were going to die there.

I suppose there might be men who would want to go to Praxis for the adventure of opening up a new world, designing and building a new society. But for most, choosing Praxis would be an option only if the alternative was even more unpleasant.

And so far, I hadn't heard many good things about the Labor Corps—.

two

"Jamie, que pasa—?"

I opened my eyes. A dark-eyed boy in a T-shirt stood in front of me. He was my age. Part of the crowd from the university. We'd all stormed out of the dorm together. José something. We'd shared a class or two.

He grinned. "I saw. You pissed on the cops."

"It seemed like a good idea at the time. What did you do?"

A rueful smile. "I threw a bottle."

"And they arrested you for that?"

"It was full of gasoline."

"You came prepared?"

"It wasn't mine. Somebody handed it to me."

"You think the judge will believe that?"

"I know he won't."

"You're entitled to reasonable doubt."

"That doesn't exist anymore. Not where there's video."

He sat down on the bench next to me.

"They swept up all of us." He waved his hand to indicate the rest of the building. "This place is filled."

"Yeah."

"You know, we're screwed."

"That thought had occurred to me."

"You got family?"

"No."

"Me neither."

"Insurance?"

"Not for this. Canceled after the Homecoming riot."

"Yeah. Me too."

He sniffed. Allergy or crying, I couldn't tell. He wiped his nose. "What are you going to do?"

"I dunno."

"I think I'm gonna option. I think Praxis."

"You been listening to Big Mick."

"Yeah." Then he added, "But Praxis has open sky. Stars. I want to see stars. Real stars. Estrellas!"

"But they won't be our stars. It won't even be our galaxy. It won't be anyplace anybody can recognize."

That was the thing about portals. The skies were always different. So different, they couldn't be identified. Even the lighthouse quasars were different. Nobody knew where—or even when—those other worlds existed. Something called Heisenberg uncertainty in the design matrices. You can design for one thing, but not the other. It's still mostly a guessing game. That's why you can open a portal to an unknown world that might be on the other side of the universe and a billion years from now, but you can't open a doorway to today's moon or Mars. Not yet, anyway. Maybe someday. If they ever figure out how to design the equations out to the ultimate decimal of pi.

José shrugged. "I don't care. I just want out." He

looked around at the bare stone walls of the lockup. "Out of here. Out of this city. Out of this whole crappy system."

I grunted. A grunt is the safest answer. It says you heard. It doesn't say you agree. Even better, it doesn't say you disagree. Disagreement is dangerous. You can get hurt disagreeing.

"You know what I heard?" I didn't answer. He went on anyway. "I heard the reason they need so many guys on Praxis, they keep losing 'em. Yeah, maybe there are things out in the scrub that eat people, but what I heard is that the climate is so easy, you can just walk off the plantation. Go off on your own, live on the beach, eat coconuts and fish, nobody to hassle you. I heard there's a lot of guys doing that. Work just long enough to learn how things work, then take off on their own."

That was interesting. "Why don't they drag them back?" I held up my wrist to show the band. "Aren't they chipped?"

José shrugged. "Maybe it's not cost-effective to go after 'em. Maybe it's just easier to bring in new. Maybe the guys who wanna leave, you use 'em for scouting and exploring or just write 'em off as a loss. I dunno. There's gotta be something. But that's what I heard. Nobody's coming back anyway, so it's all just stories. But what if it's true? A place beyond the walls? That would be real freedom, wouldn't it?"

"I'm not sure anyone knows what freedom is anymore," I said. Having finally said it aloud, the words startled me. What did I mean by that? What did anyone mean?

José fell silent. And I was left thinking about freedom. I couldn't define it, not in words, but I didn't feel free. I didn't think anybody did anymore.

My situation—before my arrest—was a good example. I had an extended education contract. As a university-sponsored consumer, I was eligible for a federal subsidy. In return for Basic Living Expenses, the subsidy required me to take seven units per term, participate in an additional two units of research or data mining, and maintain a 2.85 or better GPA. Was that "freedom to learn"—or was it "assigned labor?" Or—as some cynics like to argue, the mandatory creation of more skilled workers for the Labor Corps.

It wasn't like I had a lot of other options. There weren't any. If you don't have options, you don't have choices—and if you don't have choices, are you really free?

That didn't matter now. Unless I was miraculously acquitted—highly unlikely, not with the video evidence—my subsidy would be canceled. Automatically null and void, under the no-strikes rule. So the only choice left was which slave camp I wanted to be sent to.

Freedom? Hah.

Compared to all that, going out into the scrub didn't seem like such a bad idea.

On the other hand—leaving Earth? Never coming back?

But then again, what had Earth done for me? It was crowded, polluted, and desperate. There wasn't any place for me here—and even if there were a place, there would be ten thousand applicants already in line ahead of me.

The argument went back and forth in my head. Yes, no, yes, no, yes, no. Unlike everything else in my experience, I couldn't detach myself from this decision, because whatever I decided, it was going to be permanent. This was a lot more life-changing than choosing between First Aid 101 and Advanced Plumbing.

After a while, I tuned out most of the noise around me. It's a necessary skill for city-dwellers, being able to withdraw inside yourself. You have no personal space beyond your skin, but you have infinite space inside your head. And if you're any good at using that space, you can explore the possibilities of actual wisdom—at least, that's what I'd learned in Basic Meditation Techniques.

One of the techniques was a very old one. Ask questions. Keep asking questions. Where does it hurt? Why does it hurt? Was there a similar hurt before this? Imagine it's a knot on a string. Pull the string up and find the earlier knot. Now keep pulling and find the earlier knot. Pull some more and find the earlier knot. Keep pulling it up until you reach the bottom-most knot.

What came up was the view from the top of the diving tower. It was too high and I was too small. I could jump off or I could climb back down. I knew I could climb back down, I'd done it before. But I didn't know if I could jump off, I'd never done that. It was an old memory. I must have been six or seven.

And as I looked at it, I realized—what I was afraid of was leaping into the unknown. I knew what life would be like in the Labor Corps. Most assignments had that same stink of ruthless regimentation. I did not know who or what I would be on Praxis. But Praxis was permanent.

José said guys went off into the scrub, lived off the land—but were they doing that because the land was so attractive? Or were they running away from something so horrible that living off the scrub was the only desperate alternative?

The arguments about emigrating were still going on—all around me. Most of them were pretty shallow. That was to be expected. Most of these guys weren't very good at research. I was. That was the skill you most needed to succeed as an education-consumer.

José was talking again.

I opened my eyes and looked at him. "Say what?"

"I know you're thinking about it. Buddy up with me. They give priority to contract families, bonded pairs, married couples, partners, even buddies—stability units they call them."

"So what?"

"They're not going to take everybody, only a few of us. If we're buddies, that ups our chances."

"I never said I wanted to go."

"But you've been thinking about it."

"I think about a lot of things. That doesn't mean I want to do them."

"You want to stay here? Be a Labor Corps slave? You do know the life expectancy of a slave, don't you? At least, on Praxis, we'd have a chance. And you have useful skills. That makes you a priority candidate. Together, we—"

I glared at him.

"I looked you up. So what? I want to get out of here. If not you—" He shrugged. He glanced around the room. "I can probably find somebody else, but you're my best shot."

"What's in it for me?"

"The difference between possibly and certainly."

Something about the way he said it. It was a good answer.

I stopped myself from replying and just looked at him. Small, wiry, clear-eyed. Mixed descent, hard to say, certainly Asian, possibly some African-American, a smidge of Caucasian, and definitely Latino. He had a California accent. That would explain a lot. But I wasn't going to hold that against him. Definitely a contract student like me. And probably very smart. He had that look—focused. And he was precise in his language. That was usually a giveaway.

And he was studying me too. "James, it's all over the web. The regressives have made the universities an issue. They're whining that it's gotten too expensive to subsidize the education contracts."

"They can't cancel the contracts. That's illegal. It's a federal guarantee. Paying people to get educated is good business. And it's good for the national economy. And even if they could, that'd just create a whole new class of unemployed, homeless, and hungry. And angry. And educated enough to make waves. We know how to vote. They can't be that stupid."

"Yeah, I took that same class. Remember?"

"So what's your point?"

"They're not going to cancel the contracts. They're just going to cancel the contract holders. Us. That's what this is about. Haven't you been following the news?"

"Which news? Which set of lies and misinformation?"

He ignored the question. He spoke very seriously now. "The Labor Corps needs thirty thousand conscripts a month. Every time they take on a new job—like the Sahara canals or whatever—that number goes up another five to ten thousand. Those bodies have to come from somewhere." He pointed around. "This is it, James. We're being purged."

"Interesting theory." But it kinda made sense.

"It's not a theory. The cops knew there was going to be a riot, they even planned it. Think about it. All those tanks, all those cops, all that riot gear, all those buses lined up. They had to be prepping for weeks. That stuff doesn't happen by accident. It was planned. The cops swept up over a thousand of us in one night. They're still sweeping. Do you know what that's worth to the city in indenture contracts? A couple hundred million— at least that much after all the bribes and payoffs. No, there aren't going to be any acquittals. Unless you have a family that can outbid the Labor Corps, you're on your way to Africa."

I didn't answer. Conspiracy theories were cheap. I'd heard a lot of them. Some of them even made sense. This one did. But that didn't prove anything either. But whether or not José was right, the outcome was the same.

"Say yes. We gotta do this. Really."

"I don't gotta anything. I don't even know you."

"My name is José Miguel Rodríguez-Chan. I am twenty-three years old. Ortho-male. Heterosexual. Unmarried. No children. I had a girlfriend for four months, but she took a job in Texas as a surrogate-programmer. I have completed majors in biology, agriculture, mechanical engineering, journalism and music. I have no brothers or sisters, my father is dead, my mother lives in Buenos Aires and doesn't speak to me because I didn't return to Argentina with her. I should have. What else do you need to know?"

"Why me?"

"Because we're both here. And we know each other. Do you want to go with a stranger?" He added, "Okay, we don't know each other all that well, but we get along well enough. We usually vote the same way at dorm-bloc meetings. And we were in the same class on Self-Sufficiency, Planning and Preparation. I sat three rows behind you. You were the smartest one in the room. Well, almost. I beat your scores a couple times. When I looked you up, I ran our psychometrics. We're compatible—seventy-eight percent. If we had time, we'd be good friends. But we don't have time. We have to decide now—before sentencing."

I took a deep breath. He was almost convincing.

But before I could say anything, the buzzer went off, the lights came up, and they were herding us into the courtroom, all fifty of us.

three

Judge Villanova looked tired and unhappy. She'd been hearing cases all day. She'd probably heard every possible story by now. We entered the court and each of us in turn held our wristbands over the security scanner. She didn't even look at us. She sat on her high bench, watching our case files roll up on her display, a sour expression on her face.

The first few cases were up-and-down. The accused stepped forward, pled guilty, and accepted a voluntary indenture to the Labor Corps. "Let it be entered." Bang. "Next?"

Then she called Shaved-Head. He stepped up to the dock and said, "I request emigration for myself and my contract-family."

She didn't look surprised. "Is your family here?"

"Yes, Your Honor." He pointed.

"Have them step up."

Tiger-Tat and one other man joined Shaved-Head in the dock. Judge Villanova had them identify themselves. She checked off their names on her display. "Are you all three agreed on the terms of your contract?"

They nodded yes. "And your choice of portal?"

"Praxis, Your Honor."

"Very well." She made a note. "Is the agent for Praxis in court?"

A broad-shouldered man on the side stood up. "Here." He wore a glistening suit and data-glasses.

"These three are remanded to your custody. You have twenty-four hours to take them or throw them back. Next case," She banged her gavel. "No talking, please."

She worked her way through several more prisoners. Then: "José Miguel Rodríguez-Chan?"

José stepped to the dock. He waved his hand over the scanner to confirm his identity. Judge Villanova looked at her display, looked at him, shook her head, and said, "I really hate sentencing contract students. You had a good thing going—"

"Your Honor?" José spoke up. "I request labor emigration. For myself and my partner."

She looked down at him. "Who's your partner?"

José turned and pointed at me. "James Patrick Dolan."

"Step up to the dock. Verify your identity."

I started to protest, but realized that she wouldn't hear my protest until I identified myself. I went and stood next to José. I put my right hand on the scan-panel. It blinked green.

"James Patrick Dolan, are you in a partnership with José Miguel Rodríguez-Chan?"

"Um—" José grabbed my hand quickly and squeezed it. The Judge looked over the top of her glasses, saw us holding hands, and made a note on the display in front of her. She looked back down at me. "I need to hear you say it aloud."

José squeezed my hand harder.

And I squeezed back.

"Yes'm," I said. Then louder, "Yes, Your Honor."

"Thank you." She frowned at her display. "I don't see a record of it here. When was this partnership confirmed? How long have you been together?"

"Six months," José said quickly. "We're in the same dorm-bloc and we were in the same class six months ago. We just haven't—It should be in your records there. Self-Sufficiency?"

"I see." She frowned. She took her glasses off, rubbed the bridge of her nose with her eyes closed, put her glasses back on, and sighed. "If this is a contract of convenience, boys—"

"No, ma'am. It's not. We're real."

"—because I see a lot of these last-minute partnerships. Attempts to avoid the Labor Corps. But I'm willing to give you the benefit of the doubt." She looked to me. "You want to go to Praxis too?"

"Uh—yes, Your Honor, I do."

She wasn't convinced. "Is that a yes-it's-a-good-idea yes? Or is that a whatever-it-takes-no-matter-what commitment?"

"Um." I looked to José. His eyes were bright. I looked back to the judge. "It's a commitment," I said. It was what she wanted to hear. José squeezed my hand tight.

"All right. Well, let's test it. Mr. Firestone?"

The agent from Praxis stood up. "Yes, Your Honor?" He took off his data-glasses.

"You have the files of these two in front of you?"

"Yes, Your Honor."

"How do they look?"

"Not bad, I'd really prefer to interview them before accepting their indentures, but—"

"If they were married, would that improve their prospects?"

"Of course, but—"

"On a scale of 1 to 10?"

"If there are no disqualifying conditions." He glanced at the tablet in his hand. "I don't see any here. We would accept them."

"Thank you." Judge Villanova turned back to us, an unspoken question on her face.

"Uh—"

José squeezed my hand again. Harder than ever. I pulled away reflexively.

"Mr. Dolan?"

"I—uh. Yeah. Um. I just hadn't realized—" I swallowed hard and tried again. "Whatever it takes, Your Honor. No matter what." I took José's hand again.

"Mr. Dolan, Mr. Rodríguez-Chan, I have the authority to marry you. Right now, in this court. Is that your request?"

We looked at each other, nervously. She was testing us. This was not what either of us had expected. But José faced her and nodded. "Yes, Your Honor." He squeezed my hand.

I took a deep breath and agreed. "Yes. It is. Yes."

"Mm. I still don't believe you. But I'm required by law to honor your request for emigration. And I'm required by law to recognize and affirm your partnership contract. If that's what you really want. Last chance to back out…?"

I didn't say anything; neither did José.

"All right." She looked from José to me. "Are you both single consenting adults? Are you entering into this contract of your own free will? Are you free of any and all previous legal obligations and encumbrances? Place your right hands on the panels in front of you—thank you."

She looked at her own display. "José Miguel Rodríguez-Chan, do you take James Patrick Dolan to be your lawful wedded husband, with all of the attendant privileges, rights, benefits, and responsibilities of the marriage contract, for—" She stopped. "Duration?"

"Unlimited," said José.

"You're sure?"

"Sí."

"Mr. Dolan? Is that your understanding as well?"

"Uh-huh, yes."

She turned back to José. "—for as long as you both shall choose, in a partnership indivisible except by mutual consent? Mr. Rodríguez-Chan?"

"Sí, señora. I do," José said.

She focused on me and repeated the same question. "James Patrick Dolan, do you take José Miguel Rodríguez-Chan to be your lawful wedded husband, with all of the attendant privileges, rights, benefits, and responsibilities of the marriage contract for as long as you both shall choose, in a partnership indivisible except by mutual consent? Mr. Dolan?"

I nodded, swallowed hard, realized I was abruptly feeling something very strange. I managed to croak out, "Yes, I do."

"You do understand, both of you, that marriage is a partnership. It's not about what you're going to get out of it. It's about what you're going to put into it. I want you to look at each other, right now. Take each other's hands—"

We did. José's eyes were wide.

"Are you committed to contributing to this person opposite you? No, don't say it to me. Say it to him."

José thought for a second, then he said, "James Patrick, "You make a difference to me. I promise to make the same difference to you."

My throat was suddenly dry. My voice cracked. "José Miguel. You—you found me. You saved me. So my life is yours."

"I've heard worse." Judge Villanova said, "Do you have rings?"

"No, Your Honor."

"Bailiff? Do we have—"

"Yes, Judge." The bailiff held up a small cardboard box. She was a big Black woman. She had pulled the rings out of her desk before the first "I do."

"Nothing fancy," said Judge Villanova. "But consider this a gift of the court."

José opened the box. Two plain black rings. "José Miguel, repeat after me. 'James Patrick Dolan, with this ring, I thee wed—'"

He slid the ring on my finger. It felt cold and strange.

"James Patrick?"

"José Miguel Rodríguez-Chan, with this ring, I thee wed—" I put the ring on his finger. He held his left palm to mine. The rings beeped and glowed for an instant. They were activated. I'd always know how near or far he was.

We turned back to Judge Villanova.

"Your marriage is now recorded and certified by the Commonwealth. You may kiss your husband."

"Uh—" I turned to José.

"Shut up," he said. He held my face between his hands and pulled me down to him. A quick peck on the lips. Then a second kiss, this one a little longer. I'd been kissed by friends before, the occasional friendship kiss, it didn't bother me, but this wasn't a friendship kiss. It was just … different.

He let me go and Judge Villanova said, "Congratulations." The bailiff, the court clerk, and Mr. Firestone echoed her. Various others in the courtroom applauded.

The clerk reached under her desk and pulled out two copies of the marriage certificate, still warm from the printer. "Mazel tov." Two seconds later, "And here are your indenture documents."

"Good luck on your emigration interview," Judge Villanova said. "Don't get thrown back. Going to the Labor Corps—that would automatically annul your marriage." Then she added, "Prove me wrong. I don't want to see you in my court again."

"Uh, yes. Thank you, ma'am. Your Honor."

"We'll see." She looked past my shoulder. "Next?"

The bailiff pointed us toward an interview room. José took me by the hand and led me out, "Come on, husband."

Four

The interview room was cold. We sat in silence. I twisted the ring on my finger nervously, not looking at José. Finally, "You think this room is bugged?" I asked.

"Of course, it is. The entire building. You can't take a shit without the court knowing what you had for lunch."

"We shouldn't be here."

"Agreed," José replied. "But as of twenty minutes ago, we're both convicted felons. In the eyes of the state, we're just a couple of commissions."

"You're scared, aren't you?"

"Very."

"What if …" I couldn't finish the sentence.

José shook his head. "I think the judge made it clear to the agent. She expects us to emigrate. She was doing us a favor, you know."

"Yeah, I know."

"You want to stay here—?"

"What I wanted was to stay in school—"

"Well, that's not gonna happen. You and I are officially separated from that career path. As of twenty minutes ago—twenty-one minutes now."

José leaned forward and took my hands in his. "James. Jim. Husband. We are caught in the middle of a coup. The only way the regressives can seize control is to get rid of as many progressives as possible. That means emptying the state-subsidized schools and purging as many of us as they can. They were going to get us one way or another."

"You can't prove that—"

"I don't have to. Look at the socio-metrics. You studied chaos-theory. This country is teetering on the edge. It's primed. One good push in the wrong direction and you can destabilize the entire structure of government. Martial law gives you the opportunity to restructure whatever you want regardless of the consent of the people. We might be the lucky ones, getting out of here now. Before it happens."

He squeezed my hands meaningfully. "Let's not screw it up in here. Let's go to Praxis."

"Okay, okay," I said. "It's not like I have a choice anymore."

"No. We both have a choice. It's this—or something much, much worse. I choose this. And you did too. Now own it."

I nodded, but he saw the look on my face.

"I know. It's happening too fast. Me too." He smiled. "I mean, I would have rather married the redhead, but he didn't get arrested."

"You mean that?"

"No, I'm joking." Then he added. "Okay, I'm not joking. But you and I have better psychometrics, so this is probably a better arrangement."

"Do you look up metrics on everyone you know?"

"Sure, don't you? Doesn't everybody? If you're going to have friends, why not have friends you're going to keep? Friends you get along with?"

"How about making friends the old-fashioned way? Because you like them and they like you?"

"And we all know how well that works out. No, this is better—"

Mr. Firestone came in then, slapping his tablet onto the desk. He took the chair opposite us and unbuttoned his coat. "I guess I'm stuck with you," he said.

"Does that mean we're accepted?"

"That's up to you." He pushed the tablet aside. "How much do you know about Praxis?"

We repeated what we'd heard in the lockup.

"That's accurate. Mostly." He glanced from one to the other of us. "I assume it's not a problem for you that Praxis is a monosexual colony."

"That's what Big Mick said. That there won't be any women." I glanced at José, then back to Firestone. "I assume that's a temporary restriction? That at some point in the foreseeable future—? When the colony is self-sufficient and stabilized…?"

Firestone studied me. "Why do you assume that? Is that something you want?"

"Well, um—" I stopped. "What am I missing?"

"A lot. The background. The big picture. The context. Everything."

I shut up and waited.

"Understand this. A colony is a lifetime of hard work. You're walking into a very strict regimen necessary for survival. Not just your own—everyone's. You get to be responsible for the well-being of the entire colony. You have to submerge your identity and your survival into the colony's identity and its survival. You get that? It's not a choice. It's a requirement."

I nodded cautiously and waited for the rest. José reached over and squeezed my hand.

Firestone continued. "But sometimes—and sometimes it's a lot more than sometimes—there are colonists who bump up against the restrictions of authority, they disagree with the sacrifices required, or they get frustrated by the rules. We try to weed those people out before they get to the portal, but sometimes we miss. Sometimes people still go through expecting some marvelous rainbow delusion of freedom—let me disabuse you of that right now. Don't confuse freedom with license. Where you're going—yeah, it's mostly a shirtsleeve world. In some places, not all. And it's not going to be easy. It won't be. There's a lot of hard work waiting for you over there. Praxis has weather. A lot of it. Most of it violent. Wind. Rain. Dust. Tides. Tornadoes. Thunder. Lightning. Hail. Hurricanes. Haboobs. Blizzards. Several active volcanoes, some of them underwater. Earthquakes. Tsunamis."

José cleared his throat, not because he wanted to speak, but because Firestone looked like he expected a response. José finally said, "It sounds ... exciting."

"It is. Or so I'm told. I've never been there, of course. But my colleagues who have gone over—they say it's exhilarating and terrifying, both at the same time. Especially if you've spent most of your life in the tunnels of a city. You may not know this—but weather used to be fatal. On Praxis, it still is."

"Um. Okay."

"But the other question?" José said. "About the women?"

Firestone's expression was unreadable. "Why do you think Praxis is monosexual?"

I shrugged. "Well, the most obvious reason—the economic collapse of Miranda."

"What do you know about Miranda?"

"What everybody knows. The colony was on the threshold of self-sufficiency, so they opened up a pilgrimage, thinking that the new labor force would push them over the top. They focused on married couples, which seemed like a good idea, but a lot of those couples wanted to start families. They went right into a baby boom. Within three years, what was it—Ten percent? Fifteen?—of the colony's resources were tied up in maternity expenses, obstetrics, pre- and post-natal care, crèches, school construction, teacher-prep, and so on. The moms and pops started voting self-interest instead of what was necessary for self-sufficiency. That was a shirtsleeve world, so they couldn't return. So the colony is on full subsidy now, with self-sufficiency at least twelve years away, not until the first wave of boomers are old enough to work. And, if I remember correctly, the carefully worked out plan for the colony has been almost completely rewritten, swamped by the votes of the later pilgrimages, all those who decided Miranda should now be a family-friendly world."

"Is that what they taught you in school?"

I nodded. "Monosexuality gives you control over population growth."

"That's not the whole story," Firestone said. "That's the cleaned-up version." He paused. "I'll tell you what happened. Not because you need to know what happened on Miranda, but because you need to know why we're not going to make the same mistake on Praxis.

"The problem with a shirtsleeve world—" He cleared his throat. "—it should be obvious. If the environment is friendly enough, you don't have to stay in the colony to survive."

"Yeah, I heard about that."

Firestone continued as if I hadn't spoken. "We call it leakage. Sometimes men are exiled from a community for anti-social behavior. More often though, the exit is voluntary. When it's voluntary, it can still be useful to the colony. We need people for scouting, exploring, mapping, surveying, gathering samples, and so on. There are a lot of things bots can do, but people still like to go out and see for themselves. As long as they're not reproducing, setting up townships in reserved areas, they're still giving us valuable information about the overall livability of the planet."

"Okay," said José. "But we're getting sidetracked. What happened on Miranda?"

"Same thing. But with a difference. Women."

"That sounds kind of—"

"It isn't. It's a fair analysis. Women change the social equation. Men change their behavior around women. Plans get sabotaged by the biological imperative. Women build nests. Men get territorial. Children get born and complicate everything. Everyone gets protective in different ways. Not just for the parents, but for everyone in their circle as well. Colony plans get subverted."

He leaned forward. "So here's what happened on Miranda. Emigrating couples were told up front to limit the size of their families. Don't have six children. The colony can't afford it. One. Maybe two if the colony is on track for self-sufficiency. But there were religious fanatics who didn't like that restriction. We didn't know that, they'd kept it hidden. It was a stealth plan. They emigrated as a group. Once over there, they announced that God's word was more important than the survival of the community that had welcomed them. As soon as they were challenged, they bolted. They went a hundred klicks upriver and started a village of their own.

"Either they didn't know or they did know and didn't care—but there was a plan in place to build a dam across that river. The colony was going to regulate the annual flow of water for crop stability and create a dependable source of electrical power for industrial expansion. But five, ten years in, the unauthorized settlement had expanded like a cancer, grown into a sprawling little town of ranches and farms, plantations and villas. The colony couldn't build the dam, it would have flooded the whole region. The settlers protested. And with all their kids counted, they had enough votes to stall everything. So the dam didn't happen, neither did the industrial expansion, and the license-holders have been struggling ever since. They don't have the water they projected, so they can't grow the crops or raise the animals they planned, they have to buy them from the upriver towns, so they're even farther from self-sufficiency than before. Meanwhile, the settlers continue to expand into new territories with larger families than ever. The place is a mess and downriver is so polluted, the original settlement may have to be abandoned."

"What do you think will happen?"

"I know what will happen." Firestone hesitated for a moment, then made a decision. "I can tell you. It doesn't matter now. Miranda's official license-holders filed an action with the Portal Authority charging that the immigrants in the uncontrolled settlements were guilty of a wholesale violation of the terms of their indenture. That was nine years ago. It took some time for the case to work its way through the Portal Authority courts, but the proceedings were finally unsealed last week. The petition for relief has been granted."

"But—" José said, "They can't send those people back to Earth."

"Don't have to. The portal to Miranda is on a barren staging world. Blackworld Mines. The disobedient colonists are going to be relocated—by force, if necessary—to a newly-opened Blackworld barracks community. They'll be reassigned to the Labor Corps. Miranda sold their indentures. The children—well, Blackworld will school them. Eventually, when all the indentures are paid off, which could take a long time, they can reapply to Miranda. But Miranda's now a decade behind schedule, and they're not going to be so trusting in the future."

"How do you know all this?" José asked.

"Blackworld is a staging world, one of the better ones. There are more than twenty active portals over there. Four of them go to worlds that can be terra-formed. Three more go to shirtsleeve worlds. Miranda, Bael—and Praxis. There's a lot of trade. We also trade information. It's useful."

"Bael? When does that open?"

"Never. Not in our lifetimes anyway. Portal Authority thinks there might be some kind of sapient life over there. We've got survey-bots watching. That's it."

I held up a hand to interrupt. "I think we're getting off-topic…?"

Firestone straightened in his chair. "No, we haven't. Not really. This is an assessment. My job is to get a sense of who the two of you are. Whether or not you can contribute to the community."

"Oh, okay—" I put my hand down.

"You never answered the question," said José.

"What question?"

"When women will be coming to Praxis?"

"At the moment, there are no plans."

"So no babies? No families?"

"Not quite," Firestone said. "There will be babies, but male babies only. Bottle-babies. And not until after self-sufficiency is achieved. Only stable married couples will be licensed for reproduction. The intention is to keep the colony monosexual. Parenting will be limited to qualified couples. Reproductive freedom is one of the sacrifices you will have to make for community stability."

"Oh." José looked over at me.

Firestone looked from one to the other of us, a question on his face. "Is that a deal-breaker for either of you?"

"Um, no—I don't think so," I said.

José grabbed my hand and squeezed it. I was beginning to recognize it as a signal to shut up. We were going to have to talk about that. Very soon.

Firestone picked up his tablet and looked at the display. "I see you're both identified as heterosexual. Nothing to be ashamed of. Fully forty percent of the male population identifies as heterosexual. Is that strictly heterosexual? Or mostly?"

"Does that matter?" I asked. This was a trick I had learned a long time ago. If someone asks you a question that makes you uncomfortable, answer it with another question.

"Not at all," said Firestone. "Let me give you the rest of this. Before we put you on a train, you're going to have sixteen weeks of training and orientation. Usually, it's longer than that, but we need active bodies onsite right now, a lot faster than we expected. Don't assume that's going to work in your favor. Completing your training and orientation will not necessarily guarantee emigration to Praxis. You will be rigorously graded— much more seriously than any course you've ever taken at the university.

"In addition to that—" He paused. "Have either of you ever undergone any adjustment procedures?"

"What kind of procedures?"

"Rechanneling, reprogramming, rebooting, reconstruction? Bonding, bleshing, melding, implanting, augmenting …" He trailed off. "Whatever's necessary."

I shook my head. José hesitated. "I've done some work, but—"

"What kind of work?"

"Um. Nothing big. Effectiveness trainings. To make me a better student. More dependable. And, I think, when I was little, my mother put me through some kind of sexual reorientation thing. She was afraid I might be maricón. I don't think I was, but she took me to a lot of different doctors. I don't know what that was all about. I think she was worried about getting me ready for school, because I was smaller than all the other kids. ..." José shrugged. "I think it's made me a little—como se dice cautious—paranoid about what other people think."

Firestone paged through several screens on his tablet. "I don't see anything about that here, but it's not a problem." He looked up. "Would you have any resistance to further procedures?"

"Uh—? What kind?"

"Some moderate community-level rechanneling is required, to assist with your assimilation into a monosexual community. There are additional recommended procedures, but those are optional. You'll get more information in the orientation, and again in the trainings, and as each option is presented. None of these are required for emigration, and all of them will be available on the other side, if you decide later."

"Like the ones you mentioned? Reconstruction? Rebooting? Melding? Bleshing?"

"Yes."

I glanced over at José. "I'm not sure I want someone tampering with my head—my sense of identity," I said. "I don't know how José feels. We've never talked about it."

"Is that a deal-breaker—?" Firestone's eyes were sharp.

José squeezed my hand. Hard.

"Uh, no. I was just—I just don't want to stop being me."

"That won't be a problem. As I understand the procedures, you will feel that you are more of yourself, not less."

"You haven't done them?"

"I'm not emigrating."

"Oh. Okay."

"Look," he said, leaning forward. "The two of you are both good candidates. I can approve you. And it's normal for men of your age to be uncertain about a lot of things. But it works out."

"Always?"

"Usually." He looked at his tablet. "In your cases—both of you—with the psychometrics you have, I see a seventy-percent confidence rating."

"Is that good?"

"It's better than most. The highest I've ever seen was eighty-two. We don't get higher numbers than that. Not because of the applicants, but because of the adjustment curve on the other side. Now, let's talk about your skillsets and how they might best be applied...."

I don't know how long we were in there, at least two hours. We talked about everything, mostly what we wanted to do on the other side and what we would be expected to do as well. At one point, Firestone sent out for sandwiches and sodas. I knew he had other applicants—Shaved-Head and Tiger-Tat and that third guy—but Firestone shrugged them off. "They can wait. They'll be useful on Praxis, yes, but we're looking for a different caliber of candidates as well. Educated. Highly educated. I could have approved you both without an interview, but—" he smiled, his first smile of the day. "—the last time I was tempted to do that, it would have been a mistake. You two look good. I'm satisfied I can approve you. I just have one more thing I want to clear up. It's not a big part of the interview, it's mostly to satisfy my own curiosity—" The casual way he said it, I knew it had to be the most important part of the interview. "—how long did you two actually know each other before you got married? Or did you just meet in the lockup? We see that a lot, you know."

José and I exchanged a glance. He squeezed my hand. I jerked it away.

"We sorta knew each other at school. We partnered in the lockup," I said. "Is that a deal-breaker?"

"No, not at all." Firestone made a check mark on his tablet. "I just wanted to know how honest you are. We're done here. You're approved for orientation and training."

"But, uh—"

He looked at me. "I don't care. The colony doesn't care. The only thing we want to know is whether or not you can be depended upon. Congratulations. Don't screw it up."

Five

We had three days to close up our dorm-cubes, sell off or give away everything we couldn't carry in a backpack and roller, and report for transportation. If we didn't show up by the end of the third day, no problem, the warrants for the Labor Corps would be issued automatically.

Firestone's instructions had been precise. "Bring only what you can't replace or import—your teddy bear and your tablet. Small pieces of artwork are encouraged. All your personal memories should fit on a card. Bring your music, book, and video collections on a second card, but be prepared to share. In any case, the colony will have datalinks back to Earth, so two-way communication will be possible. Don't worry about clothes or personal grooming supplies, those will be provided onsite, just bring what you need for the trip west."

We didn't take the full three days. We had a quick dorm sale. We didn't know if we'd need money on Praxis, but it might be good to have some in our accounts anyway. What we couldn't sell, we turned over to a reclamation company for a flat fee. We didn't talk much about our marriage, there wasn't time. We made abrupt goodbyes around the university, it was easier than trying to explain, and were on the train west a day and a half later. Too fast. It was all happening too fast.

Both of us were exhausted. José leaned against me and fell asleep almost immediately. I thought about pushing him to the other side so he could snore against the window, but … I didn't. He wasn't that hard to put up with. In fact, I had to give him credit, he was pretty good at being a partner, even a husband. Better than me, so far. I hadn't finished being cranky.

On the other hand, I didn't have to worry about mid-terms anymore.

Out the window, the shuddering city slid away into the past. We clunked across the bridge, over the river and through the factories. The faded suburbs disappeared in their turn, and then we were moving swiftly through landscapes of brown and yellow and even a bit of green here and there—reminders of the world that used to be and possible predictions of the world we hoped to see.

Packing, selling, abandoning, rushing, running for the train—I'd felt conned and manipulated. Also confused, angry, put-upon, frustrated, upset, annoyed, pushed, pulled, beaten up, beaten down, tired, stressed, ugly, and a few other emotions I had no names for. I suppose I could have looked them up in the dictionary.

Yes, I'd been interested in emigration. Everybody was. And yes, I'd dreamt of a beautiful sunset over a tropical beach on a shirtsleeve world. Who didn't? I just didn't want to get there this way. I wanted—.

Actually, I didn't know what I wanted—.

But now that the train was hurtling west through a bleak starless night—.

I started laughing.

For the first time in my life, I felt free.

Why was I worrying? I didn't have exams. I didn't have crowds. I didn't have anything. I was leaving it all behind. I had a ticket to Praxis and a husband snoring softly on my shoulder. He was smart and he bathed regularly. I could live with that.

Lots of guys married guys. It was convenient. It was a rung on the ladder. Partnerships were evidence of stability. Partnerships were conducive to advancement. It was a career path and a political commitment. Evidence of social responsibility. I'd considered it. I'd even been asked a couple of times, but the psychometrics were below optimum and I'm not desperate. Wasn't desperate.

At least, José was tolerable in his own intense way. It was almost nice, having him next to me. The way I'd heard it, having a husband was like having a puppy. You can expect a puppy to pee on the carpet, but asleep they're adorable— and awake, they can be fun to play with. A husband, however … I dunno. Everything else I've heard, they're harder to train.

On the other hand, I wasn't the most lovable pooch in the litter either. If I thought about it, I had to be a little surprised that José chose me. I wasn't the only contract student in the lockup. But … I was one of the smartest ones. José wasn't the only guy who knows how to look things up.

José woke up bleary-eyed, climbed over me, and stumbled off to the lav. Eventually he stumbled back, looking marginally fresher. "Come on," I said. "Let's go get some coffee."

I dragged him forward to the restaurant car and plopped him into a chair. He sagged forward and braced his head in his hands. I punched for coffee and sandwiches. "You okay?"

"I will be. Thank you."

We sat in silence until the bot slid into position above our table. It lowered a tray between us. Two coffees. Two sandwiches. Condiments, napkins, spoons. I held up my wrist for the bot to charge me, it beeped appreciatively and slid away.

José grabbed one of the coffees, popped its top, and sipped carefully. "Ahh."

"Which sandwich do you want? Ham or beef?"

He shrugged. "I don't care."

"Might be the last ham or beef we'll see for a while."

"We have sixteen weeks." He grabbed one of the sandwiches, looked at it. "Ham. I'm good." He unwrapped it, took a half, and bit into it. "Maybe there'll be ham and beef on the other side...?"

"I'm not counting on anything. If rations are thin, we'll be eating soylent." I started unwrapping the other sandwich. It was fresher than I expected.

"You're a good husband," José said abruptly.

"Thanks. You too."

He looked across at me. "Did we make a mistake?"

I thought about it. I thought about it some more. "We didn't have much choice."

"No, we didn't." He took another bite. "It's just—I'm sorry I forced you."

"You didn't force me. I chose."

"I pushed you hard."

I shrugged. "You had to."

"Still—"

I held up my left hand, showing him the ring. "See this? I let you put it on my finger. Yeah, it was sudden. But I chose it."

"Okay," he said. He took a bite, chewed sullenly. "What?"

"This wasn't the way I wanted to get married."

"Oh?"

"I was raised in Argentina. Old-fashioned. You know? Marriage is a holy sacrament. A lifetime commitment. Two people. In love with each other. Usually a man and a woman, but not always. But at least, they're in love." He looked across at me. "This is a business arrangement. A marriage of convenience. You know it. I know it. The judge knew it."

"You're unhappy?"

"I'm as happy as I can be ... under the circumstances."

"Okay." My turn to chew silently. I sipped at my coffee to cover my reaction. I didn't know what I was feeling now. Hurt? Disappointed? Relieved?

"Okay," I said. "After we get to Praxis, maybe we can get annulled."

"Is that what you want?"

I shrugged. "Is that what you want—?"

He shrugged. "Let's just ... make the best of it for now, okay?"

"Okay. That's what I was planning anyway."

We finished our sandwiches in silence. I didn't think he knew what to say either. I didn't like feeling this way. We're supposed to be partners.

Finally, I had to speak. "Look, it could have been worse. A lot worse. You could have ended up with Tiger-Tat. I could have ended up with Shaved-Head?"

"Tiger-Tat? Shaved-Head?"

"My nicknames for Leon and Alexei. Remember?"

"Oh, them. Yeah." He allowed himself a smile, a small one. "Yeah. They kinda deserve each other, don't they?"

"And the third guy, I didn't catch his name."

"Me neither. Maybe he's the middle of their sandwich?"

"Yick. I don't need that picture in my head."

"Sorry. I minored in Sexual Politics." He laughed, a soft liquid chuckle. "Okay. We're in this together. Let's just do it. I'll watch out for you, you watch out for me. We'll go to Praxis and make it work. Whatever it takes."

"Sounds like a plan." I reached across the table and put my hand on his shoulder. He was trembling.

"Are you cold?"

"No. I'm scared."

"Yeah, me too. Let's be scared together."

SIX

Orientation and training turned out to be a lot less fun than we expected it to be.

We began each day with stretching exercises, then a jog around the camp—not my thing, jogging, but they played music like the fast parts of the *William Tell Overture* and the *Dance Of The Hours* and that made it even less fun.

It wasn't about how fast you ran, it was about finishing, it was about commitment, so it didn't matter how long it took to get around the track, which was a little over a mile. By the third day, it was about encouraging everybody to keep up with the group. We fell into four or five different clusters, ranging from the slowest to the fastest, but nobody ran alone, we all had running buddies. José and I were in the middle group, although sometimes we fell back to encourage those who were slower than us.

After the jog, there was a half hour of calisthenics. Jumping jacks, crunches, rope-climbing, and an obstacle course of tires and hurdles and scrambling through mud. After the mud, we hit the showers. There were over three hundred of us. The youngest was fourteen, the oldest was over seventy—a diverse bunch, all shapes, all sizes, all colors. I heard six different languages I could identify, English, Spanish, French, German, Chinese, and something Scandinavian, and a few more I couldn't place.

There were a lot of couples, several contract families, a few cluster-groups, and a lot more singletons than I expected. Maybe José had overstated the case for marriage, I didn't ask, I don't think either one of us wanted to talk about it yet. Maybe we could have made it on our own—but then again, we didn't know how many single applicants had been rejected either. Maybe these guys were the extraordinary ones, or maybe they had critically important skills.

At the end of the day, it didn't matter. José and I were married. We were here.

After showers, breakfast. There was no breakfast until everybody had completed every exercise and showered. The rule was everybody goes or nobody goes. We couldn't go to the next part of the training until everybody was complete in this part.

Breakfast was simple, but hearty. Eggs, toast, harvested-bacon, pancakes, hash browns, orange juice, coffee, tea. If as a group, we'd beaten our own record around the track, or if we'd pulled a hundred percent in an important exercise, there would be strawberries or waffles and a couple of times, huevos rancheros and eggs Benedict. Once we had a full English breakfast, which startled almost everyone. Baked beans? Fried tomatoes? And what's this black thing?

The same applied to lunches and dinners. The more progress we made, the better the meals got. The trainers warned us though, "Don't expect meals like this on Praxis. Meals like this take hard work. If you aren't willing to bust your asses, you're going to be chowing down on soylent and cardboard."

After breakfast, we were put on work teams. Each team rotated through a series of jobs. Cleaning, cooking, laundry, gardening, farming, weeding, planting, harvesting, tending the meat-tanks, construction, plumbing, wiring, supervising, and even managing. Everybody had a turn as a team leader. That was interesting—it was amazing how incompetent most of us were dealing with each other. We didn't know how to listen to authority, we didn't know how to be authority. We didn't create the relationships necessary for producing results.

Before lunch, another trip through the showers—this time, decontamination routines, usually just high-pressure sprays of soap and water and foam, but every so often we were subjected to actual decon and detox agents. The idea was to get us accustomed to an obsessive-compulsive level of personal cleanliness. Despite all the vaccinations we were getting every week, the best defense against infection is not being exposed to it in the first place.

After lunch, debriefing—what had we learned during the morning's work, especially about our interactions with each other. It wasn't a bitch session—it was a rigorous clean-up exercise. What misunderstandings did we need to straighten out? What perpetrations, failures, and upsets had to be acknowledged?

Who needed to apologize? Who needed to ask forgiveness? Who needed to get off their goddamn high horse and accept the apology offered? Sometimes that was interesting, more often it was a bore. But very quickly, we learned a lot about ourselves—how we reacted, how we behaved, how we screwed things up for ourselves and the people around us. Eventually, we even learned to respect each other.

This isn't to say it was all touchy-feely. Most of the time, it wasn't. Most of the time it was about results—and the trainers could be aggressive to the point of abusiveness.

"You're here because you screwed up. You're assholes. Accept it. Because if you don't own it, it owns you. Once you admit you're an asshole, we can start training you to stop acting like assholes. And once we can trust that you know how to function as a real community, maybe, just maybe, some of you will get to Praxis. Maybe. It's not a promise. It's only a possibility. Until then, you're assholes."

That was the first day. After that, it got worse.

"Do you really want to go to Praxis? Or are you just in here to jerk us all off? It's not just your survival that's at stake on the other side—it'll be the survival of every person who goes with you! Look around—that's every other person in this room! Their survival depends on you! How do you think they feel about you being a fuckup?

"And there are several thousand more already over there who you haven't met yet, but who will have to trust you not to be stupid. They're trusting you'll be ready for the challenges when you arrive! I'm not sending them any losers! Give me half a reason and I'll kick you out of here so hard you'll starve to death before you stop rolling!"

We had our share of dropouts. We started with three hundred and fifty. We lost nearly fifty the first week. Nobody was officially kicked out—the technical term was *they selected themselves out.* As in, "It was always their choice. By refusing to accept the level of personal responsibility necessary for survival on Praxis, they selected themselves out."

It was like the jogging—something I hated from the first morning, and a little more each successive morning—grit your teeth and keep going. It wasn't about how fast you were going, it was about how hard you were trying to complete. If you said, "Aww, fuck it all. I'm not running—" not only would you not get breakfast, but you'd find your belongings packed and waiting for you by the time you got back to the dorm. We saw that happen several times the first week.

They didn't exactly encourage us to drop out. They just didn't want to waste their time on anyone who couldn't make it. "You think this is too hard? Okay, leave. There are no fences here. You can walk away any time you want. Nobody will stop you. Nobody will come after you. Nobody will care. The Canadian border is only eighty-seven miles north, but a lot farther to the nearest town on the other side and I don't know how glad they'll be to see you. Nobody's ever made it. So far, nobody's gotten more than thirty-six miles, that's what the tracker said, but it could have been the part the wolf ate. Dunno. But nobody's going to stop you from trying, maybe you'll be the first."

Every aspect of the training was deliberately intense. And finally, one morning, I'd had enough. I was physically drained, emotionally too—and one morning, it finally caught up with me. I don't know why then and not before. I only knew I was tired, my feet hurt, my legs hurt, my ass hurt, my back hurt, my arms hurt, my chest hurt, my face hurt—I felt weak and exhausted, it hurt to breathe, my throat was sore and every gasp of the bright morning air rasped like cold fire. I could barely lift one foot in front of the other. I stopped. I put my hands on my knees, I croaked out, "This is not worth it."

That's when José came back and said, "Don't quit now! Just a little farther!"

"It is not just a little farther! We're not even halfway!"

He didn't argue. He pulled me upright. He got behind me and started pushing. Then someone else came up on my right, and a third person on my left, and while they didn't exactly drag me along, they made damn sure I couldn't quit either. "Come on, just take two more steps, three more, that's it. Come on! You can do it. Come on!"

But José was the most ferocious: "You do not get to bail! If you get kicked out, so do I—and I am not going to let you fuck it up for me! We are not going back! You made a promise, you fucker, and you're going to keep it! Now keep going, you lazy asshole!" I cussed at him the whole way, inventing several new swear words in the process. But he just kept pushing me. Every time I tried to stop, he pulled me up and pushed me again.

I ranted, I raged. I didn't have the energy to call him everything I was thinking. I just stumbled forward, determined to get away from him. When we got back to the dorms, I was going to punch him so hard his gramma would yell ouch! If I'd had the breath, I would have invented a whole new language just for cursing. I was still raging even as he dragged me into the showers and pushed me under the water, shorts and all. I swallowed a mouthful and started choking. And then, for reasons I still can't explain, I started crying. José held me against him while I blubbered. A couple of other guys stepped in close and put their hands on my shoulders too.

I wasn't the first person to break down crying in the first or second week. I wasn't the last either. I choked out great racking sobs of anguish and frustration and release until I was so weak I would have collapsed to the floor if José hadn't been holding me up. I was so weak I didn't have the energy to die. I just wanted to catch enough breath so I could tell him how much I hated him. And then, finally, I pushed him away, peeled off my wet shorts, turned to the wall, and washed myself in silence, not looking at anybody, not saying anything. Feeling stupid, embarrassed, empty. Drained.

Nobody said anything as we went into breakfast, but a couple of fellows patted me on the back reassuringly as they passed ahead. And then José put his arm around my waist, and I put mine around his shoulder and we just walked the rest of the way together. "I told you I'd take care of you," he said softly.

I bumped him sideways a little, leaned on him a bit more, my way of saying thanks without having to speak the words.

A couple days later, it was José's turn, but that was a whole other kind of moment.

seven

After the debriefing sessions, we had a different kind of training. Discovery, Breakthrough, and Effectiveness. These sessions could take anywhere from four to six hours and they were about how to be a more effective human being. There were several trainers for these sessions too. The Senior Trainer was an older guy named Whipple or Whittle or something like that, but everybody called him Perfessor. Perf for short. He usually worked with two junior trainers and a staff of assistants who sat at the back of the room.

Perfessor warned us on the first day that these sessions were deliberately designed to test us. Parts of the training would be uncomfortable, parts might be liberating. The training was not therapy, but some people might experience it as therapeutic. It could be cathartic. During the course of the trainings, we could expect to feel apathetic, resigned, despairing, sad, afraid, resistant, and angry. We would probably be bored. We might find parts of it interesting, possibly exhilarating. We might even rise to enthusiasm and passion. But it was our responsibility to manage ourselves, no one else's.

Perfessor was patient and literate and purposeful. He said he was going to push us hard, but always started the same way, "Who wants a breakthrough?" And he wouldn't start the discussion until we were all agreeing to it, even demanding it. And then, once he had permission, he'd lead us into some very difficult emotional territories. He might fix a person with a look that would have them feeling transparent and exposed, but it was soon clear that he was committed to the success of every person in the room. He wanted us to win.

At first, most of us thought the training sessions would be a relief from the harder physical work of the morning. They weren't. They were just as aggressive and there were days when we trudged into the training room with reluctance. It didn't matter that we would usually end the session energized and renewed—getting there was as rigorous as running around the track.

Every session was structured the same way. Perf would begin by giving us a distinction to consider—like "what you resist, persists." Then we'd do an exercise that would have us experience that distinction. Then we'd have the opportunity to share what we were discovering about ourselves.

Perf didn't settle for the easy answers. He demanded that we dig deep and discover, because discovery is the key to breakthrough. "How did you react to the process? What did you feel? What judgments did you make? Where did those judgments come from?"

He delivered his questions in a deceptively soft voice, but his words sliced like a scalpel. "What are you discovering about yourself? Is that who you want to be? What are you willing to give up? Who are you committed to being? What support are you willing to accept? Don't sell me another plate of the same old bullshit that you used to scrape by out there. This isn't out there—and we don't eat bullshit on Praxis! I want to hear the stuff you're *not* saying. The stuff you'd rather die than speak aloud. Because until you drag that shit up and acknowledge it and own it, it's going to own you. It's going to keep running you around and around the track over and over and over again, so many times you'll think exhaustion is normal. Who wants to be exhausted every day? Raise your hands? Nobody? Then why aren't you cooperating with the process of your own training— this is where breakthrough happens!"

He said that so many times and in so many ways that pretty soon we could all have the same conversations with each other. It didn't take long to figure out that was his intention—to train us to demand excellence from each other, but mostly from ourselves.

One afternoon, Perf whirled on Leon—formerly known as Shaved-Head—as if he'd heard the skeptical expression on his face. Leon had been holding back, we all knew it, but nobody had called him out. Not until now. In the middle of a sentence, Perf stopped himself and turned around to confront Leon. "Knock it off. You're a phony, a fraud, a pretender, a ridiculous performance of strength designed to hide just how big a coward you really are. I am not fucking interested in your judgment that this is all some silly airy-fairy, touchy-feely, let's all sing kumbaya together, set of whyte-flavored bullshit. I'm interested in whether or not you're the kind of person who can build a colony. You're going to break through in here because it's too dangerous to have you break down over there!" Perf went on in that vein for a while, long enough that we were all squirming. Leon stopped talking for three days, and when he did start talking again, he wasn't the same. He was … nicer.

The hardest sessions were those on communication. The trainers hammered us relentlessly on our inability to be clear.

The most important skill, Perf said—necessary for everything else—was accurate communication. And, he continued, based on the evidence, our failure to achieve even a semblance of accuracy was why we were failures. Oh, and assholes.

True communication is the act of taking an experience out of your own self and sharing it with another, evoking it so vividly and so accurately that they will recreate it and understand it for themselves. And most human beings have never learned how to do that.

Perf had us play a game called "Russian Telephone" to demonstrate just how incompetent we were at communicating. It's a kid's game, everyone lines up and the leader whispers a phrase to the first person. He whispers it to the next, and each person passes it on in turn. What comes out the other end is nothing like the original saying.

That was embarrassing.

Perf explained that true communication only occurs when a specific set of transactions has been fulfilled—something that most of us don't do, because we're operating on the assumption that knowing how to talk is the same as knowing how to communicate. Speaking is broadcasting, it isn't communication.

According to Perf, communication can't be complete without an acknowledgment. A simple "copy that," or "I got it," is usually sufficient. But sometimes it's important to check that the communication was accurately received. The first person can say, "Repeat it back to me, please." Or the second person can ask, "Say again?" or "So what I'm hearing is …" And this can go back and forth until the transmitter is satisfied that the receiver did hear the message correctly.

The next time we played "Russian Telephone," it took a lot longer—but the phrase came through unchanged.

We thought we had accomplished something.

But no.

Perf still wasn't satisfied.

All we had accomplished was only an accurate transmission of the message. But true communication isn't about exact transmission, it's about accurately decoding the meaning.

He put it on the board. How many different ways can you decode "Time flies like an arrow." Are we talking about flies as a verb or flies as a noun? Was time a noun or an adjective? Look at all the different ways you can decode those four words. He had fun with that. I'm not sure we did. We laughed, yes, but the point was that true communication is about *understanding*. What did the other person *mean?* He might not have used the most accurate words, but could you still decode his intention? What was the intention behind the communication? What result was it intended to produce?

That triggered a lot of … heated discussions. Not just in the session, but anywhere two or more people were talking. Every time there was confusion of any kind, we turned into junior-Perfs, analyzing, interpreting, and decoding each other until we either reached a conclusion or everybody was exhausted.

And that wasn't the half of it.

Perf said that the real problem was that none of us knew how to listen.

But he didn't explain that one, not right away. He told us to go off somewhere and figure out what real listening was.

"Talk to each other. Not with the intention of being heard, but with the intention of what you're hearing. Really hearing."

eight

So, for a couple of days, we all just grunted at each other, reluctant to speak, afraid to be heard, unwilling to be analyzed, self-conscious about what we might be revealing.

But it was too late. We already had a pretty good idea of each other. We'd started to figure out each other's patterns of behavior. And a lot of it was getting tense. The idea that all of us were responsible for all of us was not a popular one. Shaved-Head said it sounded like collectivism. Not sure where he learned a word that had more than two syllables, I was even more sure he didn't know what it meant—but I wasn't willing to say that to the group because that was the kind of remark that, as José was quick to point out when I shared it with him, demonstrated arrogance.

But in our late-night bull sessions—appropriately named—some of us did try to figure out what real listening was. By then we'd had enough of that thing that Perf called "context" that we were able to fumble our way toward a bit of understanding.

Listening is about getting it. Whatever it is.

The particles of listening—particles, that's another bit of Perf's annoying jargon, sometimes it felt like we were learning to speak Martian—the particles of listening don't have names. They just have questions.

Where is the other person coming from? What's the context of their communication? Their communication is not about you, it's about what they see—so what is that person revealing about themself? If you listen long enough and hard enough, you can hear what they're not saying—but that's a skill that only comes when you shut up and hear.

After a few days, Perf asked us what we'd learned about listening.

Not everybody was in agreement, but a fellow named Dennis stood up and summarized our late-night discussions in a single sentence. "It isn't about listening, it's about hearing."

"Anything else?"

"No," said Dennis and sat down.

Perf nodded and said, "Okay, yeah." started to turn away, then turned back and said, "Yeah. Some of you figured it out. Give yourself some applause. Okay, that's enough. Don't overdo it. You're still assholes."

By then, we were starting to consider "assholes" as a term of endearment. No longer an insult, just an appropriate description of inappropriate behavior.

"Look," said Perf. "Yes, we've talked about what you have to do to communicate accurately. Some of you are even trying to do it. And some of you have figured out that the other part of communication is listening. And some of you are even trying to do it. But there's a third part. Most of you are still transmitting bullshit. That's why you're assholes."

He paused, looked around at us. All of us. "Yes, we are monitoring you. Twenty-four-slash-seven. And we're not happy. You're still a long way from where you need to be. Praxis needs hard workers, yes. Praxis needs men who are well-trained and responsible for the well-being of the whole community—but right now the colony isn't so desperate as to take any of you. No matter how well you think you're doing, you're not. You think we're being affectionate now, when we call you assholes. We're not. We're disgusted. You still haven't learned to behave like a community. You're still an uncoordinated rabble. And I can't fix that. You have to. Because the alternative is … well, you know what the alternative is."

A fellow named Tyler stood up then. "So how do we fix it?"

"Take responsibility," said Perf.

Tyler shook his head. "You keep talking about responsibility. Self-awareness. Communication. All that shit. But you never tell us what to do, how to … how to do it."

"Because I can't do it for you!" Perf snapped. It was as angry as we'd ever seen him. "The best I can do is …" He sighed. He stopped himself. He took another breath. "I'm not going to Praxis. You are. Maybe. I'm just another blind man carrying a lantern so others can see. What we're doing in here, I don't want to fail. But much more than that, I don't want you, any of you, to fail. Because that will cost lives. Yours and others."

The room fell silent. Tyler sat down. Perf returned to his chair at the front of the room and sank into it. He shook his head wearily. "I hear you," he said. "I really do.

I understand your frustration. I've been there myself." He took another deep breath.

"Okay," he said. "Let's try this. Let me give you a technical term. It's a very precise term, although most of you don't realize just how precise it is. But you use it anyway. The term is … 'bullshit.' Yes, it is a technical term. It defines a specific act of speaking.

"It's not some vague judgment for characterizing things you don't like or things you disagree with. It has a precise definition.

"Bullshit is *lying*. Bullshit is excuses, justifications, rationalizations, manipulations—all the stories you make up to duck and dodge your own responsibility in the matter. Bullshit is the abrogation of responsibility. And that's why all of you are full of shit. Because you keep trying to separate yourselves from accountability."

Perf got off his chair then and strode to the center of the room. He whirled around, pointing at all of us. "*Your* bullshit is an insult to the people around you. It's a way of saying, 'I don't respect you enough to be honest. I think you're so stupid that I can lie to you and you'll believe it.' How many of you like being lied to? Levanten sus manos. Raise your hands. Nobody? So if you don't like it, why do you do it? Why do you think anyone else likes it? How many of you want to put up with other people's bullshit? Levanten sus manos. Raise your hands. Nobody again? So why do you think other people want to put up with *your* bullshit?"

He let that sink in for a moment. "Yeah—you want to notice what falls out of your mouth. It isn't pretty. Mostly it's self-righteous, self-centered, self-justification. You want to know why I'm disgusted with all of you? We analyzed your speaking. Everything since you got here. More than ninety percent of what you say is bullshit.

"Before we can send you to Praxis, we have to get it down to—oh, I dunno—let's say ten percent. Low enough that the people around you don't want to kill you anymore. And yes, I'm talking to you, Leon. And your butt-buddies too."

That was the short version. There was a lot more, because Perf had to say it at least six different ways before it started to sink in.

Myself, I just stopped talking. I became so self-conscious about what I might be saying, I didn't want to say anything at all. But I wasn't that much of a talker to begin with, so I don't think anyone noticed. And I wasn't the only one who fell silent either.

But Perf had shoved time bombs down our throats and sooner or later, they were going to go off, all of them, sometimes in the training room, sometimes after hours. And most of the time, the explosions were unexpected.

José surprised all of us. Mostly me.

Perf was still talking about bullshit. But now he was confronting individuals in the room. "So let's talk about all the bullshit you're guilty of. What are the lies you've been telling—yourself and others? What did you make up to justify your petty thefts and perpetrations? How did you rationalize your behaviors? What are the excuses you've been hiding behind? What did you say and do to manipulate others so you could get what you wanted? What are all the stories you told to get here? Let's hear it. What's the bullshit you've been spreading?"

And that's when José exploded.

"I didn't fucking manipulate anybody!" José stood up and shouted. "I didn't have to justify it or rationalize it or—or—"

Oh, crap.

I put my head in my hands. I didn't know whether I was embarrassed for José. Or for myself. Or … both of us.

"Oh, really?" said the Perfessor. "You might want to take a look at your husband there—"

"He's—he's—" José grabbed me. "James, look at me—"

I looked up at him. I'm pretty sure my eyes were red.

"I didn't manipulate you—" he shouted. "I—I—told you what the options were—"

One of the junior trainers handed Perf a tablet. He glanced at it, nodded, handed it back. "Really?" he said. "Did you look up the probabilities?"

José started to shake his head, then admitted. "Yeah, I did."

"Interesting." Perf crossed the room to stand in front of José. "According to our records, both of you were eligible, both of you would have been approved, married or not."

"That's not true—"

"Do you want to look at the chart? Alec, bring back that tablet please?" Perf took it, held it in front of José. "Any questions?"

"Yes, but—I didn't know how many applicants there would be. And I knew that our chances would be better if we coupled—"

Perf looked around at the rest of the room. "How

many of you heard that as self-righteous, self-centered, self-justification?"

Almost every hand in the room went up. Including mine.

"Look around, José. There's your feedback. If one person calls you an ass, that's one person's opinion. If three hundred people call you an ass, it's time to buy a saddle."

"That's just—"

"You don't have to convince me of anything—" Perf stopped him. "I don't care. This isn't about looking good. It really isn't. You manipulated James. You know it. I know it. Everyone in this room knows it." He paused. "And James knows it." He leaned forward, looking deep into José's eyes. "Is there anything you want to say to your husband right now—?"

José looked down at me, blinking. His eyes were shining.

"Stand up, James—" Perf suggested. I did. "Go ahead, José."

"James, I—I—" And then he bolted from the room.

Perf looked to me. "Are you going after him?"

He didn't have to ask. I was already scrambling up the aisle, into the lobby. José was already out of the building. The outer doors were just sliding shut. I ran for after him, shouting. He ignored me, heading toward the farms. "José, goddammit! Don't you dare run away from me—!"

I heard more footsteps behind me, probably staff members. Maybe a couple of other emigration candidates. I didn't look. I was thinking—*I don't need all this drama. After the jogging, now this—this is going to get us kicked out for sure! And why am I chasing the little bastard anyway! He tricked me into marrying him—.*

And then I caught up with him and grabbed his arm and he stumbled and I tripped over him and we both went tumbling over each other, rolling over on the ground, with me ending up on top of him and he punching at my chest with both fists, until I grabbed his wrists and pinned him. "Stop that. Just stop it!"

He said a lot of words in Spanish then. The only ones I recognized were gringo and pendejo.

"I already know I'm a stupid white person. I married you, didn't I?"

And that's when he started choking and sobbing. "I'm sorry—I'm so sorry—lo siento mucho—"

"Yes, you dumb fuck, you manipulated me! You conned me! You told me a story! But do you really think I'm so stupid I didn't know what you were doing? I knew what you were doing. And I knew why too. You were scared of the Labor Corps! So was I. And yes, you were right, I was your best choice—and you were mine! You think I didn't look you up too?"

"I cheated you!" he said.

I slapped his face. Not too hard, but hard enough to get his attention. "No, you didn't! I chose you! I knew what I was doing. And I'm sorry I didn't tell you this sooner. I'm sorry I let you believe you had conned me."

"You're just saying that—?" But he said it without conviction.

"I made a promise to you. The same promise you made to me. I'm going to take care of you. And we're getting off this planet." I let go of his wrists. "Unless you've changed your mind." I got off him and pulled him to his feet.

José glared at me, not knowing whether he should be angry, hurt, or embarrassed.

Nearly a dozen others were watching us, but from a slight distance, mostly classmates. A couple of assistants kept them back, giving us space to sort it out ourselves.

"I feel so bad about it," José said. "I've been carrying this around. I knew I shouldn't have done it, but I was scared not to." He looked at me. "I'm so sorry. I should have been honest with you."

"Yeah, you shoulda. And I shoulda been honest with you. But we didn't know how. Not then. Now, we do—don't we? I mean, we're learning, aren't we?" I offered him a hand.

He looked at my outstretched hand, but didn't take it. "Did you mean it? What you said? You knew I was… working you?"

"Yeah, I knew it. And while you were working me, I was playing you—so we're even, aren't we?"

He screwed up his expression into not-quite-a-frown, considering it, considering everything.

"We're a couple of jerks, aren't we?"

I shrugged. "Yeah. But we're going to Praxis."

"How do you know that?"

I pulled him close and whispered into his ear. "Because we just showed again that we're honest."

It wasn't our last argument, but it was our last dangerous one.

nine

After dinner, there was always an evening session about the portals, about Blackworld, and about Praxis.

Blackworld was the scorched remains of a planet. Its star had exploded a few hundred million years before, leaving only an airless burned-out core—which made it perfect for mining a lot of the heavier stuff. It was also a great staging world for other portals.

Most new portals are targeted to open onto planets, but sometimes there's a miscalculation and a new portal gets opened below ground, or onto empty space, and once even into the heart of a star. Sometimes the situations are disastrous, so it's safer to open a new portal from a staging world where it doesn't matter as much if you blow a hole in the landscape.

There's another issue with portals that most people don't realize. The pop-media calls it meta-galactic positioning, but that's just wrong. The actual terminology is a long string of symbols with a lot of Sigmas and Deltas and Omegas of various sizes— beyond my math skills. But what it means is that portals have to have a neutral energy balance.

Planets move, they rotate, they wobble. They orbit elliptically around stars and the stars themselves are rushing through space, caught up in a galactic whirlpool that is itself spinning on its own belligerent course. There are sideways, retrograde, sidereal, and surreal velocities expressed every which way, and all at the same time. Tracking the galactic orreries is the kind of math problem that makes super-computers weep. I'm not kidding about that—quantum computers require super-cooling. The condensation on the pipes drips into catch basins. It's called "weeping." Look it up.

Funny thing—there's just a little smidge of wiggle room in the equations, something that annoys the physicists a lot. In practice it means that the delta vee match from here to there doesn't have to be exact, it only has to be close enough that it can be managed. Otherwise the portal creeps slowly across the landscape.

So energy has to be pumped from one side to the other to keep the portal balanced. Sometimes this means pumping gas or water through, but sometimes the portal is so rigidly balanced it requires a near-perfect trade—for every gram going this way an equivalent amount of mass or energy must go the other way. Earth exports a lot of sea water and CO_2 to balance its energy deficits. Or the other way around. Earth imports a lot of fresh water, nitrogen, O_2, and other useful elements.

In one of the after-dinner sessions, the speaker was a crisp-looking man from Ottawa. His name was Markham and he was darker than me.

Markham said that we should be proud. We were part of a grand adventure. Human beings leaping to the stars. It was a privilege to be a portalnaut.

Somehow the conversation drifted sideways from there. Why were we going to other worlds? Why weren't we focusing on restoring Earth?

Markham agreed. In fact that was the goal of the portal program, the restoration of a balanced bio-system on Earth. Someday there would be enough colony worlds established that half the world's population could emigrate to new frontiers. This would reduce the hypercritical stress on Terra's existing biosystems.

Someone asked, "But wouldn't that just push the problem onto the portal worlds?"

"It might seem like it," Markham said, "but the math suggests that the number of portal worlds is infinite, or at least beyond our ability to calculate accurately. Suppose we decide that the optimal number of humans per world is—oh, let's say a hundred million—we would need only 120 portal worlds. Given that only one out of ten portals will likely open onto a shirtsleeve world, we'd have to open at least 1200 portals. At the current time, we've got nine staging worlds, twenty more second and third-stage worlds, and 135 working portals opening from those stages. Forty of those working portals open onto mining or factory sites. Nineteen more portals go to worlds suitable for colonization. Twelve of those are considered "shirtsleeve." Six of those have self-sufficient habitats or settlements on track to self-sufficiency. Two more are under surveillance for future development. Right now, there are a million human beings living on other worlds, almost half of them in permanent settlements. So we still have a long way to go. But it's possible. And where it's possible, it's usually inevitable."

Tyler raised his hand. It was usually Tyler, of course.

"Excuse me, but the math doesn't work."

"Say again?"

"The math, it doesn't work."

Markham met his gaze. "Why do you think that?"

"Well, based on some of the things that we studied—before we were, *como se dice*, 'invited' to join this program—based on the ecological simulations, this planet, Earth, should really not have more than one billion human beings. It's amazing we've survived this far. Even three billion would be okay, we've learned how to manage enough key resources, but to get to that number, we'd have to emigrate at least fifty million people a month. More than that, a lot more, if you want to make a real dent in the population. People here on Earth are making six hundred thousand new babies a day. That's a lot faster than you can ship people out. What are we emigrating right now? A couple thousand a day? It's obvious, there aren't enough portals, there aren't enough self-sufficient colonies, and there aren't enough portal trains. Way not enough."

"No, not yet," said Markham. "But eventually. There was once a time when people didn't think we could build enough roads to handle fifty million vehicles a day."

"Uh-huh," said Tyler. "All of them lined up bumper-to-bumper, creeping along in a slow-motion traffic jam. You want to deport a billion people? Ten billion? What if they don't want to go? What then?"

"You're going."

"We didn't have a choice. None of us did."

"Not true," said Markham. "You chose Praxis."

"Because the alternative was worse—"

Markham cut him off. "Thank you, Tyler is it? Thank you, Tyler." He waved him back down. "I appreciate what you're saying, but we're getting off topic. I'm here to talk about Praxis. Let's do that."

Yes, he changed the subject. He didn't change the facts.

Later that night, when we were crawling into bed, still trying to figure it all out, José suggested, "Maybe all that stuff about emigration, he was just trying to make us feel part of a larger commitment. Humans colonizing the stars, right?"

"Yeah, well he should have said that. That other stuff wasn't very convincing."

José grunted what could have been agreement. He rolled to face me, hugged me, then rolled back to his side of the bed. And that was the end of that conversation.

But yes, Praxis.

Praxis is weird.

It's an oblate spheroid—which means its squashed, flatter at the poles. It's not extreme, it's not a discworld, but it's almost enough to be visible from space. We have satellite pictures.

Praxis takes a year and a half to circle its star. It has an orbit that is just elliptical enough to be annoying. At its nearest approach, twice in every orbit, it dips just enough inside the Goldilocks zone to pick up a lot of heat, but at the farthest point of its orbit, it slips outside the Goldilocks zone to give away that heat.

That's not the worst of it. Praxis has a rotation of 63 hours and 33 minutes and 12.7 seconds. This means that midday on dayside can produce temperatures high enough to turn water into steam. Midnight on nightside, not only does that steam turn back into ice, so does a lot of the carbon dioxide in the atmosphere.

What fun.

And yet, Praxis is considered a shirtsleeve environment because the hours bracketing dawn and dusk are within the zone of human habitability. If you don't mind the constant windstorms. Praxis does have native life, plants, animals, things living in the seas as well. There are vast jungles and forests hiding in the spaces between the jagged mountains. Somehow life on Praxis has adapted to the extreme conditions. The plants curl up to resist heat and cold. Most of the animals burrow, but some of them have figured out that heat and cold are just fine, especially in the oceans where constant migration is necessary.

Not exactly the paradise that was promised, but there are some relatively survivable places in the temperate zones, and that's where we were most likely headed.

There is a long waiting list of geologists, ecologists, meteorologists, and other specialists who want to emigrate. And probably a few paleontologists too. Praxis is an incredible research opportunity. Any planet is, but Praxis is more so. So yeah, there's a waiting list. Very long. As soon as Praxis is able to support several colonies of researchers, they'll start emigrating, large crowds of them. A whole new world to explore? Praxis will be an opportunity for scientific discoveries of all kinds, probably for generations.

The models suggest that the total possible habitation level before stressing the existing bio-system will peak somewhere around 15 million. Long-term, after we figure out the necessary balances for survival on the planet, that number could go up. But some people think even 15 million is too many.

At the moment Praxis paid its portal deficits mostly with ice and light-energy from its primary. Perhaps someday Praxis might also export various foodstuffs, but not while the shirtsleeve quarantine remained in effect, and that would probably not be in my lifetime.

After all this, Markham said, "Praxis is an experiment. You have to be aware of that. And not a very popular one either. You have no idea how much resistance there is to the Praxis license. There have been over ten thousand gender-discrimination lawsuits filed against this colony."

"That sounds like an expensive day in court—"

"It won't be. The colony's lawyers have moved to have all those separate cases compiled into a single class-action suit. That will require ten thousand plaintiffs and their lawyers to agree. We estimate we'll be into the third generation by then. And the whole case is moot anyway."

"Really? Why?"

"Because the Yola license has been awarded to a matriarchal system—also monosexual. If we lose, they lose before they even get started. So … there's going to be some serious pushback to those lawsuits. You don't need to worry about it. It's not going to affect your training or your emigration."

Markham wasn't the only speaker. There were others who had been studying the data coming back from the colony. They were more specific about the details. That's when things got really interesting.

Praxis was hot. Heat was energy. Energy expressed itself as motion. High energy flows into areas of lesser energy. The process is basic physics: Evaporation. Humidity. Temperature. Air pressure. Wind. Ultimately storms. Big ones. Very big ones. Hurricanes. Tornadoes. Dust storms. Haboobs. Not to mention Arctic blizzards and whiteouts that could last for months.

The summer and winter cycles were severe enough to raise and lower sea levels by as much as two meters. During spring and autumn the tides were severe enough to keep long stretches of coastline treacherous for both sailors and landlubbers.

Calling Praxis a shirtsleeve world was merely the polite way of saying, "It won't kill you quickly. It's going to beat you up first."

Vicious storms circled the polar regions all year long. The scorch belt girdled the equator with temperatures so high, the air was unbreathable without a cooling mask. Between the poles and the equator lay two bands of tundra, forests, savannah, more forests, jungles, and a variety of high and low deserts. Roaring winds scoured both hemispheres. Lightning strikes were commonplace. Firestorms were common. Rain came down so heavy you could drown just looking up. Hailstones were large enough to knock a man unconscious.

Oh, and the gravity was uneven.

Praxis was kinda squashed. It wasn't a disk, but it wasn't a sphere either. It was an oblate spheroid, misshapen enough that mapping it was the kind of challenge that kept surveyors from sleeping well. Satellite photos showed the world as flat on top and bottom with a noticeable bulge around the middle.

This meant you'd weigh less at the poles and more at the equator—except, you probably wouldn't survive either environment very long, even with survival gear. But even in the habitable ranges, you would experience some noticeable variation in the pull of Praxis' gravity.

What fun.

Vehicles on Praxis were large, heavy, and shaped like turtle shells so as not to present a high profile to Praxis' strong winds. Buildings were dug into the ground, roofs were thick and dome-shaped, often covered with at least two meters of soil and root-grass. Coastal stations were established only on high hills. Nothing was constructed in the lowlands.

There were native plants and animals on Praxis too. Discovering all the various species and how they survived was so exciting that Praxis had a waiting list of botanists and biologists eager to emigrate. The geologists and meteorologists were lined up right behind them. A few astrophysicists too.

But most of those researchers were going to have to wait for this wave of colonists to build the support systems for scientific research. We had to construct barracks to live in while we constructed power stations, fabrication facilities, communal habitats, community centers, factory-farms and processing units, storage domes, medical facilities, and finally research bases. We'd have to bulldoze roads, build a few bridges, dig some tunnels, and gather resources and raw materials for all those jobs. Even though most of our infrastructure would be constructed out of rammed earth and carbonite-foam, we'd still need a lot of raw carbon to foam. Later on, when we could start fabricating heavier machinery, we'd start foaming ceramics and aerogels and aggregates of all kinds. But Praxis would probably never have skyscrapers.

We'd dig downward instead and build groundbreakers and tunnel-enclaves. It would be years before we'd have enough resources for big science.

I suppose all of the above would have seemed dry and boring to most people, like another dumb documentary on one of the science channels. But to those of us who were planning on emigrating, it was important, even fascinating.

We began to look forward to those seminars. They became challenges. Every point raised was questioned. "Why are we doing it like that? Wouldn't it be more efficient to—?"

And every question was answered. "Because these are the only available resources right now," or "It's a working compromise until we know more about the long-term weather patterns," or "That's an interesting idea. When you get there, suggest it. Maybe you'll have the chance to test it."

A fellow named Hunter suggested that we start compiling an idea book. Almost immediately a committee of volunteers joined up and they recruited Alec, one of the assistant trainers as an advisor.

One of the first questions that came up was a critical one. "Won't the colonists already over there resent us for coming in with all these new and different ideas on how to run a colony?"

"Maybe," Alec said. "Maybe not. The settlers already in place will have their own plans and goals and ideas, already in process. You'll want to recognize that. You'll want to respect it. And it's very likely that you might not be the first emigrants to make these suggestions. If they seem obvious to you, don't you think they'll be obvious to those already onsite. And it might be that the colonists are already ahead of you. Way ahead. You'll want to respect the experience of those already in place.

"Now, listen," he said, "They'll be glad to have you, but in their eyes, you're going to arrive as liabilities, nuisances, noobs, and babies that need to be watched carefully until you learn how to take care of yourselves and survive on your own. You can't go rushing in ready to remake the world. You're going to have to take the time to learn just what kind of a bitch Praxis can be."

ten

Praxis might be a bitch, but it turned out a lot of us were bastards.

All the so-called team-building exercises only brought out the worst in us.

There were fights, a lot of them.

Leon (the Asshole Formerly Known As Shaved-Head), Tigre (Tiger-Tat), and Pear (that was they called him, I never found out his real name, but it was a pretty accurate description of his shape) were at the center of some of them. They'd walk into a room together and someone would say, "Leon and Tigre and Pear!" and the rest of the room would respond, "Oh myyyy." Pretty soon, it was just "Oh myyyy," without the set-up.

It would have been tiresome, except watching Leon explode in rage was hysterical. You didn't have to habla español to recognize that his entire tirade would have been one long bleep anywhere else. Tigre was no slack either—but it was usually Pear who threw the first punch. For a short guy, he was nasty. How he'd survived this long with that temper was a mystery.

José and I usually stayed out of the way, but some of those fights turned into free-for-alls, and when that happened, the whole team was held accountable. Not punished—*shamed*. And then we'd go on soy rations for three or more days.

Most of the smaller fights were over by the third week. A lot of guys got selected out, but a lot of residual tensions remained and those showed up mostly during team-building exercises. We'd be separated into teams, sometimes as few as five, sometimes as many as fifty, depending on the exercise. Inevitably, especially on the larger teams, cooperation would break down into arguments between the most stubborn team members. Even when the exercise was held in complete silence, the gesturing and posturing and headshaking could get ferocious.

The trainers and the rest of the staff never intervened. They always stood to one side, watching us try—and usually fail—to work things out, until finally the buzzer would go off because we had run out of time. Or if it was a different kind of exercise, someone would click a stopwatch and announce we'd taken forty-three minutes, just to turn the rug over.

That was a frustrating one. Put everybody on a small rug, green on one side, red on the other. Without anyone stepping off the rug, turn it over. That one, Leon and Tigre and Pear got so frustrated, they announced it was impossible.

The trainers and the staff immediately stepped onto the rug and demonstrated that it was not. They took nine minutes.

"You've done it before," Pear accused.

"Yes and no. We've all done it before. But not this specific group of trainers and assistants," said Perf. "The difference is that we've learned how to be a team—when to give instructions, when to follow them. That's something that none of you have learned yet. The evidence is on the stopwatch. Forty-three minutes and twelve seconds."

That night, in the barracks, during the inevitable rehash of the day's events—and who was most to blame for the fuckups—we had the worst brawl ever.

The cameras captured a lot of it—until someone climbed up on a chair and started bashing at them with a hammer. A lot of tools came out that night and José and I realized that this brawl had been planned. These tools had been stolen from the morning's construction project.

I wasn't exactly sure what the fight was about or what it was supposed to prove, but apparently Los Patriotas had decided that Las Gringas (their name for the homosexual men on the team) deserved it simply for being public about their affections.

Las Gringas had mostly kept to themselves, but after a few rough encounters, they speculated openly that Leon and Tigre and Pear (oh myyyy) were themselves maricónes—and that Leon and Tigre and Pear's cubicle should be renamed El Armario.

That made the fight inevitable.

That was Leon's fault as much as anyone else's. He was stubborn and self-righteous. And it didn't matter how aggressively Perf and the other trainers kept working with him, trying to get him to see that he was the source of his own troubles, Leon wouldn't see it. He kept trying to bully people.

But that stuff was just the tip of the doucheberg. There was a lot more underneath that nobody knew for sure. Rumor had it that a gang of Los Patriotas had tried to rape one of Las Gringas, but I'd also heard the rumor the other way around as well. And another rumor said that a couple of Los Patriotas had been caught in the showers late one night enjoying each other, or maybe enjoying a couple of Las Gringas. That story had a lot of names plugged into it, even mine and José—which was more amusing than annoying.

Whatever the case, El Armario-Habitantes were not happy—and Perf's attempts to defuse the situation in the training room had only brought all the simmering animosities up to the surface.

As soon as the fight broke out, José grabbed my arm and started pulling me toward the nearest door. "¡Vámonos!"

But before we could get there—two big guys with claw hammers blocked our way, one of them slamming José in the chest with the flat of his hand. "No way, José!" They weren't part of Los Patriotas or Las Gringas, but this fight was going to be a big one, with something for everybody.

Before José could speak, I was already stepping in between them. "Leave him alone!" I said, so loud and so deep I surprised even myself. I was already clenching my fists in readiness. I knew I was going to get the crap kicked out of me—but I didn't care. Whatever happened, they were going to know they'd been in a fight. A lesson I'd learned as a kid—if you come home with blood on your hands, make sure it's the other guy's.

Even if you lost, you made the point, and he's not going to come after you again.

Something in my stance, or my expression—the two guys turned away. The bigger one pointed off to the side. "Hey, there's Tyler—" And we were forgotten. Now it was my turn to pull José toward the door—

But by then, fire-retardant foam was coming down on all of us, thick mint-smelling billows of wetness, great sheets of it rolling down across the entire galley, smothering everything and everybody, turning us all into a polar landscape of cursing white lumps. No matter how hard I tried, I couldn't wipe it out of my eyes, more just kept pouring down. It didn't sting like pepper spray, but it wasn't fun either.

Security teams—this was the first time any of us knew that there were security teams at the station— arrived then and began separating us. They were dressed in black armor and carried nightsticks with taser-points. Some men were still trying to fight, they swung at the guards with hammers or chairs. It didn't work. They didn't have much traction in the slippery foam and they couldn't see very well anyway. The security guards came in like a wall. They tasered anyone still trying to resist, knocked them to the ground, rolled them over, and cuffed their hands behind their backs.

They frog-walked all of us outside to stand in widely-spaced ranks across the lawn. We stood cold and wet, embarrassed and ashamed. José moved sideways to stand closer to me, that's what partners are supposed to do, but one of the more overzealous guards didn't like what he saw. He came striding over, raising his nightstick—and without thinking, I barreled into him, knocking both him and me to the grass. And then everything went screeching white and red—and I was jerking across the lawn, unable even to breathe, let alone scream—

—came to, rolled in a fetal ball, raging and terrified. José was holding me in his arms, rocking me, making sounds I couldn't understand. I gasped for air and clutched my belly and somewhere in there I realized I'd pissed myself and crapped my pants and probably vomited too. I stank like a cesspool. How José could bear to put his arms around me and hold me, I couldn't understand. I didn't even want to be next to me.

By the time I recovered enough to sit up, the entire class was out on the field, shivering in the darkness. Most of us were still dripping with foam. I grunted in pain. All my muscles were still stinging and ringing. José hugged me closer to him and whispered, "Hang in there, James. You're going to be okay."

The black-armored guards had moved off to form a perimeter around us. They watched us warily. Some of the men sat down, others remained standing. We stood or sat or sprawled exhausted on the grass for more than an hour. Nobody said anything. Once or twice, someone started to protest, but quickly fell silent if any of the guards started to approach. I hadn't been the only one tasered.

After a long frustrating wait, Tigre began to shout. "They can't taser all of us! What are we waiting for? There's more of us than them—"

Half a dozen others yelled for him to shut up. "They're gonna start with you, asshole!"

That protest died quickly. The guards hadn't even moved.

Eventually, I recovered enough to stand. The grass was too cold and wet. I was shivering in pain. José helped me up and we leaned against each other. His arm around my shoulder felt warm.

Finally, Perf and all the other trainers and staff came out of the main building. They walked over with grim expressions and stood in front of the group. Perf had a tablet in his hands. I couldn't see what was on it, I assumed it was a list. He walked up one row and down the next, looking at each person in turn.

Sometimes he'd pause. He'd look at his tablet. He'd look the man in the eyes. He'd think for a minute. Then he'd make a decision. Sometimes he'd move on. Sometimes he'd raise a hand and gesture to the guards. When he did that, two or three guards would march in and escort the man out of the group. They'd take him off to the side, to a place where everyone could see those who were being selected out.

When he got to Tigre, he didn't even pause, he just pointed. Four security guards strode in. They grabbed Tigre roughly and dragged him out of the ranks. Perf kept walking. He pointed at other members of Las Patriotas without pausing. Each time, guards came in and took the man out. Perf pointed at Pear. Then Leon. The group on the side continued to grow. The two guys with claw hammers who'd accosted José. And some of Las Gringas as well.

When he got to me and José, Perf stopped and studied us. His expression was grim. I got the feeling he was having trouble deciding. After all, I'd tackled a guard. I was still hurting—and stinking. But I met his gaze, unashamed. Unafraid. *Go ahead. Do your worst.* José still had his arm around me. He felt good.

Finally, Perf made a decision. He shook his head, and kept walking.

When Perf finished walking the rows, he returned to the front. "Anyone else? Last call. Anyone else want to stand over here?" He pointed at those who'd been selected out. After a moment, three of Los Patriotas walked over. Then two of Las Gringas. And finally a couple of other men as well. Perf noted each on his tablet.

Then he waited. The moment stretched out. Finally, when it became apparent that no one else would leave the ranks, Perf turned to those he had selected out. "You have each been charged with and found guilty of incitement to riot. Your original indentures plus the ones we have added tonight have been sold to the Labor Corps." Tigre shouted something about the right to appeal, but Perf said, "There is no appeal. You waived your right to appeal when you signed your emigration contract." He gestured to someone out of sight and a large, black bus with bars on the windows rolled up behind the group. "Your belongings are already packed and aboard."

As soon as the bus rolled away, Perf turned to the rest of us. "You assholes!" he said. "You fucking assholes! What the hell is wrong with you? Every single one of you knew something was up—but not one of you stepped up to try to stop it. That alone should disqualify the whole lot of you from emigration. You weren't thinking about the team. You weren't thinking about the community. You weren't thinking at all!"

He started to turn away, then turned back. "Yes, we need people on Praxis, but we're not desperate. All of tomorrow's sessions are canceled. And the mess hall will be closed until further notice. Whatever you think you've been doing here, it isn't working. Your team is broken. You have until this time tomorrow to fix it. If you can't fix it, we'll bring in more buses."

"Can we shower first?" someone called.

"I will not discuss strategy with you," said Perf. He walked away, followed by the other trainers. The security team and several staff members stayed behind to observe, but we were no longer under guard.

For a moment, everyone hesitated, uncertain. Then the group started to break up. Most headed for the dorms and the showers. José asked me if I felt well enough to walk. I grunted. My throat hurt, I guess from screaming. I didn't remember it all.

José walked me into the showers and helped peel me out of my clothes. A couple others helped us. I was still so weak, I couldn't stand up by myself. José had to help me dry off. Mostly I just wanted to collapse into bed, but a couple of guys came by, rounding everyone up for a meeting in the training room. I didn't feel very well, I didn't want to go—but I pulled on some shorts and a shirt, leaned on José, and we followed everyone across the yard to the training room.

Inside, several people were setting up chairs. Others were taking a head count. A few others were fiddling with the lights and the sound system and the thermostat.

"Everybody settle, please—?" Hunter raised his voice to be heard. He stood at the front of the room. His face was dark. "Let's get started." He looked around.

Most of us were looking anxious, annoyed, or resentful. "Look, I know it's late, I know we're tired, and I know that I have no authority to lead this group, unless you choose me—but I do have some management skills from the business sector and if there's no objection, I'm pretty sure I can facilitate this. But if there's anyone else who wants the job—?"

Most of us had a good sense of Hunter. He'd established himself as a dependable strength on the farm and construction teams. I had no objection, but someone in the back raised a hand and said, "I'd like an election."

"Okay—" Hunter looked around. "Let's see if we can do this quickly. If we do a whole nominating process, with all the necessary seconding and everything, we'll use up a lot of time. So let's do this instead. Anyone who wants the job and thinks he can handle it, come on up here and we'll take a vote—" He looked around. He waited. Nobody stood up. He waited a little longer. "—and I guess that's the election. Thank you. Let's go to work."

Someone handed him a microphone and he nodded his thanks. He tapped it a couple of times to make sure it was on, then turned back to the rest of us. "Okay, here's how it looks to me. This is our training. Not Perf's. It's ours, and we have to own it. We have to stop waiting for them to do it for us. Because they're not going to. That's the point.

"They're not coming to Praxis with us. We're going to be on our own, so we have to be the team. And we have to start now." He took a breath. "So let me just say it. We fucked up. Seriously. We. Fucked. Up.

"We knew there was tension in the group. We all did. But none of us did anything about it. Nobody. What if this had happened on Praxis? People would have been hurt. Maybe even killed. And whatever community we might have been trying to build—it wouldn't recover. Really."

Hunter looked around the room. "And let's face the ugly truth right here and now. There is still a lot of unresolved tension in this room. We have to start there."

A few people grumbled and a lot of hands went up, you could see the arguments forming like storm clouds, but Hunter waved them back down. "Yeah, I know—we could have a bitch session. We could take turns justifying ourselves and arguing whose fault it was. We could get sucked into unsubstantiated rumors about whatever it was that might have happened in the shower room—we could do that, but if we did, we'd just be doing more of the same shit. We've been dividing ourselves. We can't afford to do that anymore. Not now and not on Praxis. Our survival is going to depend on each other."

Again he waved the arguments back down. "Please, let me finish this. Put your hands down. I know you want to open this up for discussion—and in the ordinary scheme of things, if we weren't under a deadline, I'd say, yeah, everybody should have a chance to speak. But there are—" He looked at a tablet someone held up for him. "—a hundred and sixty-six of us. Less than half of what we started with. If each person takes three minutes, and there isn't a person in this room who can limit himself to three minutes, it'll be dawn before we finish. That's not going to be the best use of our time.

So I want to suggest something else. An exercise that'll move us forward. Any objections?"

A couple voices called out. "Let's do it." Others joined them. A few people applauded. Hunter was good at enrolling people.

"Okay. It's a mingle. Just like in the afternoon trainings. We take ten minutes, fifteen, more if necessary. Everybody goes around the room and forgives everyone else. Just like in the training room. 'I give up the right to resent you. I give up whatever story I've been carrying around. I promise to build a future of partnership.' Aaron, can you put that up on the board please?" Aaron was one of the fourteen-year-olds.

Hunter repeated the phrase for Aaron two or three more times, then turned back to the room. "If this is going to work, we all have to go to the people we're most upset with. And people, please—this is not about telling your story one more time about why you're angry or upset or hurt. That's more of the same. This has to be about letting go of whatever it is you're angry or upset or hurt about. Until we clean up that shit, we can't build anything good on top of it. We can't move forward while we're still at war with each other. And we know how to do this. We've been doing it in the training room. Now let's do it for real." He looked around the room. "Any questions about the exercise? Only the exercise."

"How is this going to fix anything?" someone called out.

"Good question," said Hunter. "Any other questions? About how to do the exercise? This is about forgiveness. Giving up resentment. Creating new partnerships. Right? Everybody ready? Begin—"

Almost immediately, José turned to me. "Jamie, mi amigo. Thank you for being there for me tonight. Gracias, mi amigo. I did not know who you were until tonight. I did not know your commitment to me. The story I had about you—that you were holding back. I give it up. I was wrong." He glanced to the board where the words were written. "I give up my story. I give up the resentment I never told you about."

He caught me by surprise. I didn't know how to respond. And my throat was almost too raw to speak. So I just reached out with my hands and pulled him into a hug. Closer than a man-hug. When we finally broke, I looked into his eyes and croaked softly, "I am sorry I'm such a jerk."

"You're not a jerk."

"Yeah, I am. I'm sorry for … not caring enough. For holding back. You're a good person, José. Better than I deserve." My voice cracked, I couldn't get any more words out.

"Don't try to say anything else." He put a finger across my lips. "We can finish this later." He stood up then and joined the rest of the mingling men. I tried to stand, sank back in my chair, and concentrated on breathing.

The mood in the room was changing. We had started grim and tense. Now we were just serious and solemn. But at least that was an improvement. I saw a few smiles, a couple of hugs. That was progress.

Not a lot of people came up to me, only a few, but most of them said the same thing. They apologized for thinking I was an asshole and promised a fresh start. I nodded in response, patted my throat, croaked a couple of words, and finished instead with a sweaty hug. Somebody brought me a glass of water and I sat there sipping at it slowly. It was too cold and it hurt my throat to swallow.

Finally the exercise ended. Hunter went to the front of the room and picked up the microphone. "Finish up, please." A few seconds later, he called a halt. "Yes, I know we didn't complete. I know we all have a lot more to say to each other. And I know it needs to be said. But there are just too many of us to do this all in one session, so we'll each have to be responsible for completing this on our own time."

He came down from the dais and stood in the middle of the group. "But let's face it, it's late. We're tired. We all need to get some rest. So here's what I want to suggest. Let's call it a night. Complete what you have to, but make sure you get some sleep. We'll get up tomorrow at our usual time, all refreshed. We'll do our jogging, we'll hit the showers, and we'll regroup here at nine ayem. Between now and then, I suggest that each of us take some time to identify what part of the problem—no, what part of the team—you're willing to take responsibility for. No, not willing. Committed. Sorry, it's late and my brain is getting mushy. But here's what I'm thinking—that each of us should come in tomorrow and say, 'Here's what you can count on me for.' I think that's where we should start. After that, I think strategy will take care of itself. Any questions? Suggestions?"

A few hands went up, but most of us in the room were in agreement with the plan—probably because most of us were just as tired and we all wanted to get to bed. A couple of questions were quickly handled. Three of the suggestions were easily incorporated. Still, it took another twenty minutes before Hunter could adjourn the meeting. We escaped gratefully.

eleven

The next morning, I was sore all over, as if every muscle had been exercised beyond endurance. José said I could skip the running, several others agreed, but I shook them off. As much as it hurt to move, I wasn't going to use it as an excuse. If we were on Praxis, I wouldn't have a choice, so I didn't have a choice here.

I came in last, but there were twelve other people running with me, cheering encouragement, including the two fourteen-year-olds. That was annoying. I'd always preferred to do things on my own.

José must have seen it on my face. After we showered, after we were back in our cubicle, as he helped me pull my shirt on, he said, "Jamie? What's going on with you?"

I shook my head. "Nothing." I pulled away.

"Poopoo del toro." He pushed the sleeve up my arm.

"I hate it when you do that."

"Do what?"

"Help me. I don't need any help."

"Excuse me? You were all over me last night."

"I could barely walk."

"Well, people want to help you."

"I'm not helpless—"

"I never said you were."

"All those people this morning, running with me. Like it was the Special Olympics or something."

"They wanted to support you."

"I didn't need—"

"James. Do you know how big an asshole you can be?"

"It's part of my charm. I can live with it."

"Well, a lot of other people can't—"

I limped over to the closet and grabbed my pants. "Like you?"

"That was uncalled for."

"Sorry. My throat still hurts a little."

"That's no excuse for behaving like an asshole."

"I don't need an excuse."

"That's for sure." Abruptly, José grabbed me, he took my pants from my hand. "James, stop a minute. Just stop."

I stopped. "What do you want from me?"

"I want you to let it in."

"Let what in?"

"Support. The whole support thing. You don't let anyone support *you!* You jerk!"

"I don't need—"

"Wrong. Twice over."

I recognized that tone of voice. I shut up. I fumbled with my shirt buttons.

José pushed me backward, to sit on the bed. He started buttoning my shirt. I moved to push his hands down, but he slapped my hands away. "See?" he said. "That's exactly it."

"What is?"

"That! Dios mio! People want to support you, that's a gift to you. When you push them away, you're insulting them. You're saying their gift isn't needed, isn't appreciated. You're saying that they can't be your partner."

"*You're* my partner."

"I'm your *husband!*"

"Yeah, on paper—" That was a mistake. I corrected quickly. "Okay, you're my husband."

"Sí! And you push me away too. How do you think that makes me feel? Like you don't want me to be your husband—because you won't even let me be your partner."

"I don't—"

"Yes, you do!"

I shut up. Sometimes there are arguments you can't win. Sometimes the only way to win that kind of argument is to say, "Yes, you're right." I shut up.

José finished buttoning my shirt. He picked up my pants again. "Lift your legs." I stayed silent while he helped me finish dressing. Pants. Socks. Shoes. He helped me to my feet. "Say gracias."

"Gracias."

"De nada."

My turn to give him a look. "But it wasn't nothing."

"You're right. It was something. And it was important for me to do it for you—but before you get too full of yourself, I did it for me too. I didn't want to stand around waiting while you fumbled through it yourself."

He straightened my collar. "Now, do you need to lean on me?"

"No. I'll be all right."

"Don't be so fucking proud, amigo."

"I'm not. I can walk."

We made our way to the training room and found our usual seats. Hunter stopped by to ask how I was feeling, so did a couple others. A couple more patted me on the back in passing. It all left me feeling very uncomfortable. There was something—

Hunter went to the front of the room and began by thanking everyone. Then he held up the microphone. "Who wants to share?"

A flurry of hands went up. Hunter said, "Okay, for this to work, everybody has to keep it brief." He started calling on people. "You, you, you, then you. In that order."

The first few people to share said things like, "I am committed to the team. Blah blah blah." Duck-billed platitudes.

—I saw what was missing.

After the fifth one, I started to get impatient. These people were just puffing themselves up. Posturing. Proving something to themselves and others. It was all bullshit. It wasn't moving us toward a real resolution.

I raised my hand, I waved my hand for Hunter's attention, but he ignored me. He pointed at three other people. Maybe it was just me, but I had the sudden feeling he didn't care what I had to say. I kept raising my hand, but he kept calling on others.

Okay, I got it.

I'd have to get his attention some other way.

It still hurt to move, but I managed it somehow. I turned my chair around to face the back of the room.

José frowned, but he saw the look on my face and then he turned his chair around too. Several people around us saw what I had done. One or two understood and turned their chairs around too, joining my silent protest.

Someone else noticed and pointed to us. "Hey! Why did they turn their chairs around?"

Hunter gave no sign that he had heard. He continued to call on people. And those others continued to share the same way. "I am committed … blah blah blah."

But even when a second and a third person pointed out that by now a dozen of us had turned our chairs around, Hunter still didn't acknowledge that anything was out of the ordinary.

Finally, it was just too much. I lost my temper. José noticed I was fuming. He put his hand on my arm, but instead of stopping me, it energized me. I stood up, turned to face Hunter and shouted, "There's something going on over here, Hunter! Are you ever going to recognize us or are you just going to keep on pretending that this crap is fixing anything?"

"You weren't called on," said Hunter. "Sit back down."

"This is how you build a team?" My voice cracked, but my meaning was clear. "By steamrolling over some of us? I thought we were here to fix it, not make it worse."

"When you turned your chairs around, you opted out of the process. You have no right to—"

"I was withdrawing my support from this exercise in bullshit."

"That's why I didn't acknowledge you. Now sit down!" Hunter demanded.

"No, I will not. If you're going to hold the microphone, then you should have owned the whole room—not just the part you agree with. I have something to say. And I have the same right to speak as everyone else."

Hunter glared at me. "Is this how you make a contribution to the team? Is this your commitment to Praxis?"

"Goddamn right it is!" I hobbled forward. "Bacon and eggs! Are we the bacon or the eggs?"

"Huh?"

"Bacon and eggs only requires a contribution from the chicken—but it demands a real commitment from the pig. Are we bacon or eggs?" I finally reached the front of the room. "This isn't about commitment anymore, Hunter. We're all fucking committed. We're here. That's more than enough proof. We've been running and cleaning and cooking and gardening and training and studying and doing all kinds of fucking exercises for three weeks now—and right now it looks like all we've done is learn a new kind of bullshit to use on each other. As my husband would say, that's poopoo del toro."

"Go back to your seat, James—" Hunter ordered.

I stood my ground. "What are you going to do? Have me tasered again? Go for it. That won't prove anything except that you can taser me. I'll just keep coming back until you're ready to listen. Look at me. I'm still here. I'm still standing. Mostly." I put a hand on a chair to steady myself.

But I wasn't the only one standing now. Some were shouting for me to sit down, but others were shouting at Hunter. "Knock it off, Hunter! Let him speak. He has something to say. I want to hear James."

Hunter must have realized he was about to lose control of the room. He nodded. "Okay, James. Have your say." He handed me the microphone.

"Thank you," I took it. My throat still hurt, my voice still sounded thick. I spoke softly and slowly. "I'm sorry for losing my temper and breaking in the way I did, but I see something going on here and—look, I'm not doubting anyone's commitment here. We're all committed. Do we really need to say that? And I don't mean to diminish what anyone has already said, but it doesn't fix anything, does it? Because it doesn't change anything. It's just more blah blah. Haven't we had enough of that?" I turned to face Hunter. "You're good at running meetings, yes—but every time you take control, then the rest of us sit back and ... what's the word Perf uses?—abrogating, abnegating, something like that, our responsibilities as individuals. It's like the chairs—"

"Huh? What about the chairs?"

I pointed around the room. "Notice? It's always the same people setting out the chairs. The chair team. But it should be all of us, each of us taking responsibility for putting out our own chair, and making sure there's a chair for our buddies too. And the same thing for taking them down. Each of us should be picking up the trash, not just the trash team. We let other people do the dishes and the laundry and the sweeping—but I say that each of us should be looking to see what needs doing and just do it and not wait until it's assigned. If you see it, do it. That's what owning the responsibility should look like."

I coughed, caught my breath, accepted a cup of water from someone and said, "This morning, a dozen of you helped me finish my run. You didn't have to, but you did, to make sure I finished. Because it was important that we all finish. A couple people told me I didn't have to run if I was hurting so bad, but I ran because if I didn't the team wouldn't have been at a hundred percent. And I think that's the point. A hundred percent is about getting the job done, whatever the job is, no matter who does it. It's about all of us owning all of it. Because that's the way it's going to be on Praxis. So over here, where I'm standing, that means I have to act as if *everything* is my job. Thank you." I handed the microphone to Hunter and started limping back to my seat.

José caught me before I stumbled. He hugged me quickly. That's when I noticed that a lot of people were applauding. Many were standing.

Hunter let the applause continue for a bit. I could see that he was taken aback. I'd given him something to think about. He met my gaze and nodded slow agreement.

"James, you're right—and I apologize. I should have called on you and I was wrong for not respecting you sooner. I was wrong. What you said—it needed to be said. Thank you for saying it so clearly." He looked embarrassed. He came down from the dais and walked over to me. "I had a plan for today. I thought we'd share for a bit, finish cleaning up the past, then we'd all separate into groups, each group taking on a specific problem— but I think you nailed it. That's not the fix we need."

Hunter passed me the microphone again and I replied slowly. "Thank you. I'm still trying to figure this out, bear with me. I think … I think we're so used to appointing committees everywhere that we end up thinking that's the way to solve a problem—form a committee—but I think that's the problem. I think that's the reason we don't solve our problems, because as soon as a committee gets appointed to an issue, everybody thinks it's handled and stops taking responsibility for their own part. We don't do our own chairs, we don't pick up our own trash, whatever. And the whole world works like that, with everybody thinking that making things work is everyone else's job. We've been giving away our participation—but what we're really giving away is our power. And then nothing happens or the wrong thing happens and all we get is another reason to complain and blame someone else. What I figured out this morning, from the run, from José, I have to be responsible not just for my part, but for the whole thing. I'm not good at giving speeches, but that's what I think is needed." I handed the microphone back to Hunter and sat down again, wondering why some people were cheering and others were applauding. The applause was probably courtesy. We applauded everybody, that was the way the sessions were run, but this seemed to go on longer than usual.

When it finally died away, Hunter nodded thoughtfully. "You know something, James? You're right. You're very right. Thank you. And I apologize again for not recognizing how much you have to contribute. And I think—" His face was shining. "—I think what you said—that's the fix. That's what we have to create, each of us. That's who we have to be. Thank you for saying it." Hunter put the microphone under his arm and started softly clapping.

Others began clapping too. Pretty soon, the whole room was standing and applauding. And cheering. And yelling. And whistling. And stamping their feet.

And then—spontaneously—last night's mingle resumed. But this time, with smiles. Several of Las Gringas went over to the few remaining members of Las Patriotas, they approached each other warily, but then they started talking and soon some of them were even laughing shaking hands. I saw a few hugs in the room as well.

José put his arm around my shoulder and pulled me close, beaming proudly. I felt so embarrassed, I couldn't even look at him. Until he grabbed my face in both his hands and planted a big wet kiss on my lips. What the fuck—?

But before I could finish being astonished, the back doors of the room opened and Perf came striding in, followed by the other trainers and the staff. Perf walked over to us and took the microphone from Hunter, then he headed to the front of the room and up onto the dais.

"Please sit down," he said. He waited. He held up a hand for silence. He allowed himself a nod and a smile. "Okay, I'm impressed. The staff is impressed. You got here a lot faster than any of us predicted. We had a little pool on you. The earliest prediction was lunch time, and that was an outlier. The rest of us were guessing sometime late tonight or even tomorrow. So congratulations. You surprised us all, you got what you needed to get and you got it on your own. It's obvious that you've been paying attention in the training sessions. You applied what you learned. Good job. Very good job.

"But now, the easy part is over—and the next few days will test whether or not you have truly escalated your commitment." He cleared his throat and held up a hand for silence. "No, no sharing right now. We have some other business to take care of first."

He changed his tone then, became even more serious. "Last night, some of you voiced the suspicion that Hunter is a plant, that he was put into your group to push you in the right direction. Some of you have been muttering that the exercise Hunter ran last night is proof of that." He interrupted himself. "Yes, we do monitor you rigorously. We told you at the beginning that we would."

"So why didn't you prevent the riot—?" Someone called out.

"Because that was your job," Perf shot back. "From the beginning, we've been telling you that your survival as a team is your job. Our concern is for the success of Praxis. That means we have to be aggressive about selecting out those who can't meet all the necessary requirements. Yes, that riot was a dangerous risk. But it was your risk, not ours, and it told us a lot of what we needed to know about you—as a group and as individuals." He took a breath. "I promise you. We're not playing any games in here. We're serious about getting you ready for Praxis. That's why I want to squelch the rumors about Hunter right now. Hunter is not a plant. And no, I did not suggest to him that he run last night's exercise." Perf looked unhappy. He pointed at one of the staffers. "Alec did."

We all turned to look at the staffers lined up at the back of the room. Alec was gray-faced.

Perf continued. "This puts me—and the other trainers—in a very uncomfortable position. Staffers are not supposed to discuss strategy with you. It's one of our strictest rules." As he talked, a low rumble of disagreement began to spread across the room.

"I love Alec. We all do." Perf continued, ignoring the groundswell of disagreement. "He's a hard worker. He's been very committed to the success of this team. He cares about all of you very much. But as much as I appreciate all the hard work that Alec has done, all of his contributions to this effort, I can't allow this precedent—" By now, the rumble had grown to a grumble, with a lot of audible remarks.

"So we're going to let Alec make his goodbyes to you, we're going to acknowledge him for the contributions he's made to this team these past three weeks, and then regretfully we'll be putting him on the afternoon bus back to—"

Abruptly, José stood up. "No!" He shouted, "You can't fire him."

Perf looked over at us, startled. "You don't get a vote on this—"

"Oh, yes we do! This is our training, not yours. We're going to Praxis, not you. And if we say that Alec stays, then Alec stays. You're only our trainer, our coach. Not our boss, not our padre. From here on in, we claim responsibility. And if we want Alec to stay, he stays."

Cheers and applause. One after another, the men in the room began standing up and shouting, "Alec! Alec! Alec!"

Most of us knew Alec. He'd always been a friendly hand on the shoulder, a supportive word in the ear, an occasional bit of advice on how to hold a hoe or a shovel to avoid getting blisters, and sometimes even the necessary demonstration of a specific skill—but most important, he was a patient and understanding listener. He wasn't just a staffer, he was our friend. The chant grew louder and louder.

Perf frowned. I could tell he wasn't happy about being challenged. I don't think he was used to it. But the noise continued to grow, the crowd grew more insistent. "Alec! Alec! Alec!" We weren't going to stop.

At last, Perf recognized he couldn't win. He took a deep breath and resigned himself to the moment. He nodded to the other trainers and the staff in the back of the room. He spread his hands wide in a gesture of surrender and smiled broadly. "I guess they're taking ownership."

Perf waved Alec forward and turned him to face the cheering room. The chanting dissolved into applause and cheers. Alec's eyes were shining and his face was flushed with embarrassment. Finally Perf held up his hand and waved for silence. When the noise finally ebbed, he looked to Alec. "Your employers just renewed your contract. When you have a team that dedicated, what do you say?"

Alec took the microphone, took a deep breath, looked out at all of us, and said, "I will not discuss strategy with you. Ever again."

Laughter. Applause. Cheers. Whistles and whoops.

Perf took the microphone back and said, "Gentlemen, breakfast is waiting. After that, we're going to accelerate the work schedule. We've got a lot of time to make up."

twelve

Usually, in the evenings, we had a couple hours free time before lights-out.

Some guys went out to the garden and sat and looked at the stars. Some went to bed early. Those who had been smokers before they came to the training camp had all quit cold turkey. Some of them went out for an extra jog or a swim or worked out in the exercise room. But most of the men eventually wandered into the lounge for coffee or sodas. Some played chess or dominoes, and once or twice a week there was a poker game.

We also had a band. Or an orchestra. Hard to define. Some of the members of the group had brought instruments with them. We had an assortment of guitars, a fellow named Dersham brought his trumpet, another guy had a beautiful, black clarinet that he had to assemble, and a third had a glimmering silver flute. We also had two violin players, three keyboardists, and two guys with drums. And maybe a couple of things I didn't have names for. Eventually, they found themselves a rehearsal room, one of the smaller training rooms, and disappeared there for an hour or two after dinner.

The rest of us, mostly we talked about the events of the day or the week. We vented our frustrations, unloaded our upsets, speculated about Praxis, and sometimes even declared our ambitions. This was too often punctuated by aggressive teasing, and competitions to see who could tell the dirtiest joke.

For the first three weeks, many of the conversations had been tense, guarded, even secretive. Although most of us had become accustomed to sharing—even sharing some of our most uncomfortable secrets—in the training sessions, we hadn't brought that same camaraderie to our evening sessions.

One night, when he finally felt it was safe, Tyler told a joke about a guy who got arrested somewhere in Italy and sentenced to a long prison term. On his first day, another prisoner approached him. "You like-a golf?" he asked. (His part of the joke required a thick Italian accent.)

"Yes, I like golf."

"Atsa good. You like-a Monday. Monday, we all play golf."

"Really?"

"It'sa good game. We all play. Tell me, you like-a bowling?"

"Yes, I like bowling."

"Atsa good. You like-a Tuesday. Tuesday, we have-a bowling."

"Really?"

"Yes, It'sa good game. We all play. Tell me, you like-a sex?"

"Yes, I like sex."

"You like-a with a boy or a girl?"

"With a girl."

"Oh, you notta gonna like-a Wednesday."

Pretty soon, "Oh, you notta gonna like-a Wednesday," became an easy punch line to almost every conversation.

Except that for some of us, maybe most of us, the joke was an uncomfortable reminder that Praxis would not have any women colonists. Not in our lifetimes if the rumors were true. Even worse, every time the subject came up, someone would inevitably say, "Oh, you notta gonna like-a Wednesday." After a week or so, that punch line became brutally unfunny. At first it just drew groans and eyerolls, but after a while, it usually earned an aggressive punch on the shoulder. The joke passed into local history very fast.

The promised availability of robosex on Praxis was a more popular topic. The nice thing about robosex is that you can pick the most attractive unit out of the line—male-ish, female-ish, whatever—and you know it's going to give you an enthusiastic ride. Whatever you want, you're going all the way, the robo doesn't care. It says, "Oh—oh, yeah," no matter what you do, no matter what you want. You don't have to look good, you don't have to worry about what it will or won't do, you don't have to worry about satisfying it, and you don't have to ask for its number and pretend you want to see it again. And if you don't respect yourself in the morning, well that's okay too—at least, you won't have to worry that it doesn't either. For a lot of guys, robosex is preferable. It's convenient. Especially if you're an awkward adolescent. I'd been there—more than a few times. Who hasn't?

It's a lot easier than trying to maintain a relationship.

I had assumed—and I assumed that José assumed as well—that the robos would probably be our primary sexual exercise once we arrived on Praxis.

But sometimes, late at night, when I was lying awake and staring at the ceiling wondering why I still felt alone and isolated despite having José snoring softly beside me, I sometimes wondered if perhaps, maybe, I don't know, but what if the guys who were satisfied with robosex as their primary sexual expression were somehow emotionally incomplete. It was something I meant to talk to José about. Someday. Real soon now. At the right time. Whenever.

More than one philosopher had opined that the normal state of human beings required not just membership in a community, but intense personal bonding as well. But there were others who were equally quick to point out that because of the evolution of our technologies, humanity stood poised on the threshold of an evolutionary reinvention.

I'd written about this for one of my classes at the university. The instructor gave me a B-minus. I hadn't said anything new. But how could I say anything at all that hadn't already been said by smarter people than me? Whatever was happening hadn't finished happening—and maybe it never would. Gene-splicing, bio-shocking, augmenting, stem-cell rebooting, organ reconstruction, personal rechanneling, and all the other methods of remodeling body and mind were creating so many different evolutionary pressures that poly-chaos theory could only predict that the catastrophic break in predictive timelines was on an accelerating approach.

Whatever humanity had been for thousands of years, it was about to become something so radically different that we would not be able to know what we were becoming until after we became it. Some people said the word *trans-human* was insufficient to describe this new condition of humanity because it suggested some kind of specific, maybe even static, condition lay ahead. But the self-renewing avalanche of developments in materials sciences, biotechnologies, genetic reconstruction, organic augments, and outlying surprises had created and were continuing to create synergistic interactions that not only triggered further research and development and application, it also spawned whole new fields of research and new possibility.

What this meant for the species was a permanent state of transformational shifts, happening at an accelerating rate. The tsunami of change was already crashing over us, sweeping us forward so fast that we wouldn't know what had happened until afterward—except that the evolutionary tsunami was likely to become a permanent condition of our species.

The underlying tectonics remained mostly unknown. On the surface, the processes of change showed up as a relentless series of culture-quakes. Individuals who could afford it remodeled themselves for enhanced physical appearance and sexual prowess, redesigning their bodies to match a desired self-image. Some men turned their skins red, grew horns and tails and pointed ears. Some women became aquatic dwellers, having their legs fused into fishtails. Heavy-construction laborers remodeled themselves into huge, muscular trolls. Ballet dancers became muscular elves.

Others showed off forked tongues or a split phallus or a physical reconstruction as a hybrid human-animal—half-leopard or man-bear or neo-primate. Some grew tails. Lizard-men grew spines and scales and claws. Porcu-people, studded with thorns, were given space even in crowded venues.

Some remodeled themselves to match characters from movies, videos, even animated cartoons. Others went with neon or animated tattoos, illuminated panels on their arms and legs and backs, enriched retinas for hyper-vision, augmented hearing, extra hearts and lungs, fiber-enhanced musculature, and more. Courtesans grew hyper-muscled vaginas to massage the upgraded members of their male clients. Likewise, male escorts augmented their tools to satisfy their trade—customers of varying gender and physical circumstance.

But those changes were only the expression of something deeper. The perception of the physical body affects the construction of the identity within—everything from bitterness and resentment to pride and aggression. But when the physical image is fungible, can be remodeled, then the self-identity shifts too. Cosmetic improvement fosters an improvement in confidence and self-image—but the new possibilities that enhancements and augments created also made for personality constructions outside what had previously been defined as the norm.

Humanity was not only redesigning itself physically, but emotionally and psychically as well. The result wasn't just a great range of possible experience, but an enlarged dichotomy between the extremes of experience. Therefore—as I wrote in my paper—

the human race was driving headlong into unknown evolutionary territory.

The instructor said that I should have written a conclusion. I thought I had. I said that we couldn't know. He said I should have suggested specific possibilities. I replied that even the best sociologists in the field had failed to come up with anything more than an informed guess. Seeing as how the instructor was one of those "best sociologists in the field" that was probably the wrong thing to say.

He looked at me sharply and explained very carefully that one of the reasons why my paper was so short-sighted was that I had not directly experienced any transformations myself. Had I ever transitioned? Had I ever had a forked penis? A vagina? Breasts? Enhanced hearing or sight? Augments of any kind? Telepathy? Hyper-muscles? Cyber-chipped?

No, I hadn't. I was raised old-fashioned.

That's why you can't understand what you're writing about, James. B-minus. Thank you very much.

Yeah, it hurt my GPA, but not so much as to put my contract at risk.

While he hadn't overtly suggested I experiment with sexual remodeling—such suggestions could be considered emotional harassment—he'd made it clear that I was stunting myself, at least in his opinion.

That wasn't the only reason I'd changed my major, I'd already changed it three times in pursuit of an interdisciplinary degree, but it was a factor. My paper had scared me. If I changed myself, what would I become? Would I still be someone I wanted to be? Would I like my new self?

Call it cowardice. I wasn't the only human being on the planet who distrusted remodeling.

A lot of students at the university had enhanced and augmented and transformed themselves. I'd seen it all around me. I might have been impressed with the physical changes, but I wasn't impressed by the behavioral changes that came with. Enthusiasm became hyperbole, followed by arrogance and self-righteousness. At least, that's how it seemed to me. And when I said I wasn't interested in hearing about it anymore, I was told I was pissing on their parade.

Okay, I'm a regressive.

That's why my emigration to Praxis was so ironic.

thirteen

Praxis was also a reinvention of humanity.

An all-male colony? To some, it sounded like an opportunity. To others, more like a prison camp. But to most of us, it represented an escape.

But after the riot, after the reduction in our ranks, after the fix-it sessions, and all the healing exercises, some of us began to consider what it might mean for us as individuals, as well as a community.

"Look," said Alec, in one of the training sessions, "The human race has a lot of history with all-male environments. Factories. Construction sites. Mines. Boarding schools. Armed services. Police. Commando teams. Merchant ships. Naval vessels. Submarines. And of course, various gay communities and enclaves. So it's not like we're going blindly into this. And yes, having said all that, Praxis is also a sociological experiment.

"Some of you have likely heard of the Uplift Inquiry—if we could redesign the human species, what would we redesign it into?

"The immediately obvious answer—the one that most of you are thinking right now—is to go bionic.

Create supermen. Super senses—hearing and sight in particular, an enhanced sense of smell as well. Super muscles so you can run faster, lift heavier objects, punch harder in fights. Super strong skin so you can't be stabbed. Super sharp nails so you can shred an opponent with adamantium claws. What else? How about cyber-telepathy and implanted microprocessors to give you superior data-crunching abilities too? Okay? Sounds good, doesn't it? But you want to notice something—all of those prosthetics could very well be an evolutionary dead end.

"We're already the apex predator. We sit at the top of the food chain. We eat everything. We've already built all kinds of physical enhancements to improve our sight and our hearing and our sense of smell. We have machines that can carry us farther and faster than any human being can run, other machines to lift and carry heavy objects so we don't have to, and no end of lethal devices for punching holes in people we decide are our enemies. Defenses? We have grenades and crossbows and tasers and nerve-agents and flame-throwers and bombs. We have bullet-proof armor and helmets and bunkers. We have defensive perimeters and radar and sonar and all kinds of scanners. Community? We have instantaneous communication and pocket computers. We have robo companions for everything from caregiving to masturbation. We have essentially mastered the physical world without having to give up the flexibility and adaptability of this—" He held out his hands, he indicated himself. "—our human bodies.

"The minute we become too specialized, we give up our biggest evolutionary advantage, our ability to adapt to any environment, no matter how extreme or hostile. That's the dead-end that some of our physically-transformed neighbors may be pushing themselves into."

He put up some slides. "Here. These are the physical modifications that some South African diamond miners are undergoing. And over here, some Alaskan lumberjacks. How about these Russian infantry? Not pretty, eh? Who wants to be a troll? These people do. Okay, it was their choice, freely made. They wanted to be hulks. That big guy there on the left—he could probably scare the shit out of a grizzly bear. I know he scares the hell out of me. I wouldn't want to be in the same room with him. But these guys you're looking at, they're efficient, they're intimidating, and they eat fifteen to twenty-five kilocalories a day.

"But they'll never make love to a human woman— they'd crush her. There aren't that many female trolls either. So they've accidentally created an environment that is mostly monosexual—their fights are usually to the death. Now, to be fair, there are some women who've adapted themselves. Here's one. She calls herself Jabba the Slut. You don't make love to her, you make love *at* her. She has multiple vaginas, some are deep enough and stretch enough for an ordinary man to climb all the way into. I hear she's very popular at troll orgies. But she can't move without help from a forklift. Why does she want to be that way? I don't know—but it was her choice, freely made. And apparently, she's happy.

"You want more? I can show you a lot of other choices. All freely made. Some might seem innocuous— like skin color or sexual enhancements. But look at these pictures, these extreme examples—these are becoming more acceptable and more commonplace. Here's the question—are these a step forward or back. Are any of these persons likely to be the next Nikola Tesla? Alan Turing? Marie Curie? Beethoven or Gandhi? And what about their children? Their grandchildren? Are we balkanizing the species—creating the possibility, maybe even the inevitability, of a whole new kind of race war?"

He switched off the slides and brought up the lights. "Praxis is part of the Uplift Inquiry. It's about discovering the next level of sentience, that's *awareness*—and the next level of intelligence, that's *sapience*. They're the two sides of the same coin."

"So why no women?"

"For the same reason there will be no men on Yola. We want to find out what the species can become without the distraction of sexual dimorphism."

"Distraction?" asked someone.

"Oh, yeah," shouted someone else. "Viva la distracción!" This got a loud laugh.

Alec laughed too, but he waited for the room to settle down before he continued. "If you feel you cannot live without women in your life, you can leave the training at any time. But the fact that you're still here, after four weeks—that suggests that as individuals and even as a group you're coming to terms with the future you've chosen.

"It wasn't exactly a choice. Not a real choice, was it?" said one of the other contract students who'd been swept up the same night as José and I. A tall gangly guy. "Not when the alternative is slavery."

Alec pointed to him. "Stand up, Bell. Yes and no. It's always a choice between there and here. You chose here because you decided here is the better choice. You can change your mind right up until the moment you step aboard the transport. You have that right. It's in your contract."

"And end up in the Labor Corps?"

Alec nodded. "Yes, if that's the terms of your indenture. And when your indenture is paid off, you'd still be on Earth. If that's what you want. And I've said it more than once—all the trainers have. The Labor Corps is the easier job. Why did you choose to be here? Why are you still here?"

"Earth is a toilet. It's crowded and ugly and hungry. I want to go somewhere I'll be free."

"Ahh," said Alec. "That's a good one. Let's talk about that. What is freedom?" He looked around the room. "Anyone? What do you think freedom is?"

There were a lot of answers. It took a while. Alec rephrased a couple for clarity and put them up on the board for everyone to see.

Not being a slave.
Not being in jail.
Being able to earn a living.
Not having anyone tell you how you have to live.
Not having external control or regulation.
Being able to say or think what you want.
Being able to read or write what you want.
Having rights. Having rights respected.
Having space to explore, discover, learn.

"Okay," he said. "That's a good list. Very good. So, how many of these will you have on Praxis?

Silence in the room. No hands went up.

"Right. You don't know. You're not sure. You know what you've been told here in the training room, but none of you have any direct experience. In fact, no one on Earth does. None of us. We only have the information that's been transmitted back. But … from that information, we can assume this much. You won't be a slave, you won't be in jail, and you won't be able to earn a living as we define it here on Earth. You will have external control and regulation, and there will be an authority defining your obligations for survival, so there is that. You will be able to say or think what you want, you will be able to read or write what you want, if you have time for that, of course. You will have your rights respected, up to the point where those rights represent potential harm to the larger community. And finally, you will have space to explore, discover, and learn—but only within the circumstances that Praxis allows." He paused, looked around. "So … based on your definitions, how much of that is freedom?"

The silence continued. "Yeah," said Alec. "Wait a minute, let me give you something else." Alec went to the front of the room. Next to the trainer's chair was a music stand with a training manual for the session. He turned a few pages. "I want to read you something. There are three types of freedom," he began. "There's freedom from—a freedom from the constraints of society. I think you've acknowledged that. There's freedom to— freedom to do what you want to do. You've listed that one too. The third is freedom to be—freedom to be who you are meant to be. You almost got to that one with freedom to read and write what you want and having your rights respected, but those are still limited by the circumstances of Praxis."

He turned the page, read for a moment, then stepped away from the music stand. "Let me give you a different definition. Freedom is not license. It's responsibility." He walked down into the center of the room and looked around at us. "Freedom is the space to be responsible for yourself—to determine your own behavior within the circumstances that are provided, to consider the consequences, and to make choices. Freedom is about having choices and choosing well. That's it. That's all it can ever be in any community and especially so in a complex technological society. Your freedom is defined by what's possible in the society you live in." He paused. "Praxis will give you some of the freedoms you listed. Some. But it will demand a corresponding responsibility. That's what you need to learn here."

He stopped himself, went back to the dais and took a drink from his water bottle. "Yeah, that's the official version. Now, let me give it to you a different way. Freedom on Praxis is the freedom to starve to death. Or work a thirty-two-hour day. We'll adjust your body-clock, of course. Eight hours on, eight hours off. That's what freedom on Praxis looks like right now. Maybe later, it'll include the chance to kick off your shoes, put your feet up, and open a cold beer. Just not right now and probably not for a long time to come. But … you will be very far beyond the reach of any authority here on Earth. For the rest of your lives." He added, "So if you are going to be happy or miserable or whatever—you will at least have that choice. And because freedom is about choice, you will have that one."

"That's not going to scare me off," said Bell. He shook his long, black hair away from his eyes. "And neither is the all-male thing. I tried it, okay? No big deal. But some of you guys keep talking about rechanneling, like it's a substitute. Like it's second best."

"Yes," said Alec. "That's what it feels like to you." He looked around the room. "How many others in here feel the same way?"

A lot of hands went up. Including mine. José thought about it, then raised his hand too.

"Thank you," said Alec. "Thank you for your honesty. Yes, Praxis is a monosexual colony. What is wanted and needed is for you to be emotionally healthy and stable, not only in the community, but in your personal lives as well."

"Yeah—" said Bell. "That's the jargon. Can you say it in dog-shit English?"

After the laughter died down, Alec said, "I like your terminology. Yes." He smiled, then allowed his expression to broaden into a grin. "Right. Dog-shit English." He nodded. "Yes, okay."

He gestured for Bell to sit down again. He walked to the center of the room. His tone became very serious. "Yes. This is an experiment. Every colony is an experiment—this is one of the most ambitious ones. So is Yola.

"A few decades ago, when the first portals were opened, when we first started moving out into portal-space, it looked like we finally had a way to save this planet. It looked like we finally had a cheap and easy way to get to the stars. Except we weren't going to any stars that we knew—or even any time we could identify. We don't know what we've got out there. We only know we've got something that changes everything." He held up a hand. "No, hold your questions. I know I've changed the subject, but I need to give you the background.

"We think there might be other intelligent life in the universe. It has to be possible—and if it's possible, then considering the incomprehensible scale of the universe it's inevitable. We're very much aware that sooner or later, we're going to open a portal that leads us directly to an alien intelligence, possibly one that is vastly superior to us. We just don't know.

"Now, even if we never find any aliens out there, even the possibility of that contact raises the single most important question that humanity has ever considered. Who are we? *What* are we? What does it mean to be a human being?"

"Who's asking?" I raised my hand.

Alec glanced over. "Eh?"

I stood up. "There's only one answer to that question: what does it mean to be a human being? *Who's asking?*" Alec waited for me to explain. Not for him, but for the rest of the room.

"A cow doesn't worry about what it means to be a cow. Life is about eating grass. It doesn't come home at night and wonder if it was a good cow that day. It just chews its cud and hangs out with the other cows.

"A human being is the only intelligence that's going to ask that question: what does it mean to be a human being? So that's the only answer. *Who's asking?* Only a human being worries about a human's place in the universe."

"Good answer," said Alec over the scattered laughter. "Nevertheless—" He held up his hand. "Settle down, please. Don't fall apart. Remember, James, this is an inquiry. Remember how an inquiry works?"

"It never ends. You just keep asking questions, over and over."

"And—?"

"And every time you ask the question, you get a new answer—"

"A new *possibility*," corrected Alec.

"Right. A new possibility."

"And the inquiry continues until…?"

"Until you get to a possibility that serves your needs."

"Right. And this project—Praxis—is one of the possibilities. Let me get back to the question—who are we in this universe? Sit down now, James. Thank you. Let's all acknowledge James."

He waited for the applause to end and continued strongly. "When the Uplift Inquiry began, one of the first answers to the question—who are we?—was a very uncomfortable one.

"We're the descendants of egg-sucking therapsids. We've got a reptilian cortex and a primate hindbrain and in some of us enough of a forebrain to make the occasional good decision. We're awash in hormones that affect our thinking. The slightest chemical imbalance— thyroid, pituitary, pancreas, liver, you name it—can affect our ability to make rational choices. Some of us like to think we're spiritual beings inhabiting meat, but too often the meat runs the spirit, not the other way around.

"We reproduce by lottery. Ten million little wigglers go racing up the fallopian tubes. We have no way of knowing which of those little bastards is going to get into the egg. It's a crapshoot. For most of our history, a woman had to carry a little parasite around in her belly for nine months before she knew if it was worth the effort—healthy or deformed or stillborn. She couldn't even know the sex of the child until it was born.

"Our infancy, our childhood, our adolescence—those are equally out of control. We're swimming in hormonal storms every moment of our lives. And if that weren't bad enough, we're drowning in a chaotic sea of information, most of it false—lies and advertising and bullshit. Insane belief systems, ridiculous theologies, spiritual rapists, phony mystics—and when you add personal remodeling to the mix, you create additional possibilities for human beings to escape into virtual fantasies that only harden their multiple disassociations from rationality.

"At best, human beings are the missing link between apes and sentient beings." Alec concluded. "The Uplift Inquiry is about asking the question, what's next? What's possible for us?"

Bell waved his hand. "So what does this have to do with Praxis not having women?"

"Everything," said Alec. "Women are the other half of the human race. Praxis is about finding out what kind of species we can be if we isolate the male part of the species. Yola is about what kind of species we can be if we isolate the female half. Do we know what we're going to discover? No, we do not. And we won't know for at least a dozen generations. But the point of the inquiry is to see what kind of species we will be if we can remove the hormonal storms, all the actions, distractions, and interactions."

Now, Alec paused. This was a serious question. "How many of you have had relationships with women?" More than half of the men in the room raised their hands. "Good. Thank you. Now, think carefully. How many of you have noticed that your relationships with women have pulled you into behaviors that you later decided were … oh, let's pick a good word … *insane?*"

Almost all the same hands went up. Followed by generous laughter.

"Look," said Alec, "This isn't about women. It isn't about men. It's about the fact that interactions between the two sexes are so much about sex and sexual identity, gender and gender roles, flirting, seduction, and even the possibility of eventual copulation, that rational interactions are pulled in a thousand different directions." He held up a hand to delay questions or comments. "You look at a woman's breasts, you look at her legs, you look at her hair, her makeup, her smile—you look to see if her eyes have that sparkle that means you have a chance. That's if she's even marginally attractive. And if she's not attractive, that's also a judgment that colors your interactions with her. To most of you, a woman is a sexual fantasy, a mommy figure, a dominatrix, a child, an employee, a boss, a slave, something to be used—or just something so alien and so mysterious you have no idea how to deal with it. And the dog-shit English truth about men and women is that men truly do not understand women—*can't* understand women. Even with all the back-and-forth transitions, all the remodelings and rechannelings that are now possible, you're still hardwired with the brain you were born with. You're never going to understand what you cannot understand. And any man who claims otherwise is either lying, stupid, or deluding himself."

He held up his hand again. "Okay, that's a little harsh. I know that a lot of you have made sincere and serious efforts to experience your own femininity. I know that many of you have a history of relationships. I've read your files. But … here you are, signed up to emigrate to a planet where you'll never see another woman in your life. What's that about? You've given up? You want revenge on the woman who did it to you? You're resigned that you'll never meet *the one?* Whatever it is, the fact that you're here is evidence that you are no longer committed to a relationship with a woman. Any woman. You need to think about that. You need to think about it long and hard. Because you need to come to terms with what Praxis represents."

A dark-eyed fellow stood up then. "May I speak?"

Alec nodded. "Go ahead, Dillon."

Dillon looked around the room. "I'm not a woman-hater. I've been with women. I even tried being a woman for a while. It didn't work for me. Guys didn't relate to me the same as they did when I was a guy. See, there's something special and different that happens between two guys. If you've experienced it, you know." He stopped himself. "Sorry. That's not why I stood up. I was supposed to be here with my boyfriend. We were approved. We were going to get married. But then—"

He paused, swallowed hard, recomposed himself. "We had this friend, a woman. I thought she was our friend. But after we told her our plans, she changed. I won't go into the whole story, it's not important, but she—she did some stuff. She made herself Joe's confidante and advisor. So instead of talking to me, Joe talked to her. He told her about all the stuff that he should have been working on with me. And she advised him on what she thought he should do—she told him it was a bad idea to emigrate.

"She meddled in our relationship and she broke us up. And when I figured it out afterward and confronted her, she admitted it. She said she didn't want us to go because she didn't want to lose her best friends. And she thought if we broke up, then we wouldn't be able to go. And see, that's the thing—she wasn't the first woman who tried to meddle with our relationship. She's just the one who did the most damage." He wiped his nose. It was hard for him to say. "I'm sorry. My point is, I want to live someplace where women like her can't get to me—a place where I can have a boyfriend or a husband and not feel like a target. I'm not against women—I just don't want to deal with them anymore."

"Okay," said Alec. "First, we're not here to vilify women. That's not the purpose of this discussion— or this colony. And second, we're not here to have a pity party about things that happened in the past. The question that you need to ask yourself, Dillon, is this one—what was your responsibility in the matter?"

"Oh, I know the answer to that. We've been doing these training sessions for how long now? A month. I had to handle that one the first week, and again the second week. I know where I dropped the ball. I didn't talk to Joe. I was so busy making plans for both of us, I forgot to ask him what he wanted. And when he tried to tell me, I wasn't listening. But … also, I don't think Joe ever really wanted to go to Praxis. Or maybe he did, but … it doesn't matter now, does it?"

"Here's what matters," said Alec. "Why are you still here? Why do you want to go to Praxis?"

"Because I'm gay and I want to live in a gay world."

"Ahh," said Alec. "Thank you." He looked around at the rest of the room. "Who else feels that way? Who's going to Praxis to live in a gay community? Raise your hands."

Almost a third of the men in the room raised their hands.

"Thank you," Alec said. He looked back to Bell, the dark-haired fellow whose question had triggered this discussion. "You see, Bell? It's complicated. More things in heaven and Earth than dreamt of in your philosophy. Let's ask some more questions." He turned back to the room. "How many of you have considered rechanneling and are open to the possibility? Especially if you met the right man?" A scattering of men raised their hands.

"Okay, let's try the other side. How many of you are determined not to rechannel, no matter what?"

Not a lot of hands went up, but a few.

José looked at me, a question in his eyes. I shrugged. I hadn't thought this far ahead.

"And one more," said Alec. "How many of you are not going to raise your hands, no matter what question I ask?"

I raised my hand. I was the only one. Alec grinned. "Gotcha."

A few people laughed. Ha ha.

I sat quietly, wrapped in my own thoughts, still not knowing which of those questions I would have or should have raised my hand for.

fourteen

And then one day, it felt different.

The work got harder, but it didn't feel harder. Whatever needed doing, there were always people showing up to get it done, so no job seemed too big or too intimidating anymore. We knew it would get done. The farms turned green, the first cucumbers and tomatoes swelled on their stalks and one night we had salads we had grown ourselves.

The afternoon training courses shifted too. The first few weeks, we'd been cleaning out the shit from our personal attics. Now—according to Perf—we were remodeling the spaces of our minds. Perf said that he was training us in "the technology of consciousness" which was a fancy way of saying "being a fuckwad is no longer an option."

A lot of the terminology sounded like Martian at first—it was jargon, but Perf always decoded it. From the very first day, he was clear about why we were assholes. "What do we keep saying in here—notice! Notice! Notice! Notice! Notice what you're doing, what you're feeling, notice the effect you're having on

"

others. Most important, notice your judgments. That endless conversation running inside your head— this one's too fat, that one's too old, this one's stupid, that one's arrogant, this one is ugly, that one is cute— you're a judgment machine, churning out opinions and judgments so fast you're not conscious of them happening. And then you have the gall to think your judgments are important. The universe doesn't care. Nobody cares. Except you. Here's the bad news— your judgments reveal your thinking. And if you could actually step back and listen to your judgments, what they'd reveal is that you're full of shit.

"Pay attention! Notice the shit that falls out of your mouths, because most of you are just pretending to be human. Until your words match your deeds, you're just another faker. In here, you will be a commitment—or you will be gone."

That was pretty brutal, and we heard variations of it almost every day for the first three weeks, but after the riot, the mood in the training room was different. Patient? Gentle? Hard to explain. But it was clear that those who weren't serious enough weren't here anymore. And that meant that the rest of us could be more focused on the tasks at hand.

Perf had been handing off a lot of the training responsibilities to the junior trainers. Alec was one of the best, he was as focused as Perf. We liked him a lot. But one day Perf started having members of the group take over—he had us running the exercises or managing the sharing. After another while, he even had us coaching each other. He said, "I'm not going to Praxis, remember? You're going to have to take care of each other. And coaching is part of it." That was interesting.

Some of us were good at it, some of us were clumsy. But oftentimes, it didn't matter. Just having someone to sit with, someone who would listen patiently while you talked something through for yourself—that could be enough. And if it wasn't, there were other things a good coach could do—like ask for coaching himself.

"It's not about getting it perfect," Alec said one afternoon. "Perfection is an ideal, not a destination. Working for perfection is frustrating, because perfection is impossible. The physical universe will not allow it. So just go for excellence. Excellence is satisfying."

There were a lot of those discussions. Alec admitted that the goal was to submerge us so thoroughly and so completely into this context that we began to think like trainers, not assholes.

Colonizing a new planet? The job had to be done by humans and not machines. Turing-class bots could handle tasks as complex as air-traffic control, race-car driving, and life-threatening medical circumstances. 95% of all Turing-class decisions were optimal and that percentage was rising a little more with every iteration, but it was that remaining sliver of a percent that still required a human eye—especially when the bot's intelligence engine had to deal with information beyond its experience.

Here in the training camp where everything had to be done by hand—cooking, cleaning, managing all the necessary numbers that informed the statistics that measured our efficiency, even picking the vegetables for dinner, all of us were confronting just how isolated we'd become from our own survival. We'd let our machines leech away the satisfaction and triumph and feelings of accomplishment that were possible in life when you actually worked with your own hands.

We had to live that experience here, become familiar with it, before going through the portal. We had to learn how to think like pioneers, unafraid of getting our hands dirty, otherwise Praxis would overwhelm us, paralyze us where we stood. We created a name for the experience. We called it *can do*. And we called ourselves The Can-Do Team.

It became our mantra. Any time a task was assigned to any of us, we all responded, "Can do." Are we going to plant this field? Can do. Are we going to dig latrines? Can do. Are we going to build a power tower? Can do. We weren't going to be intimidated—not by the size, not by the difficulty. We were The Can-Do Team.

And then one day we noticed that our numbers were thinning again.

We talked about it over dinner. Most of our dropouts had "selected themselves out" in the first or second week—mostly when they realized that Praxis would be a 24/7 obligation just to survive. The Labor Corps would be a lot easier—ten hours of work, six days a week. Three meals a day, two hours of recreational time at the end of every work-shift, access to robosex on the weekends, and a warm bed every night, all guaranteed by the Geneva Convention. Plus you would get work credit for every new skill you learned, which might someday be valuable after your release. Considering all that, the Labor Corps didn't look like such a bad deal anymore.

The big brawl of the third week had cost us another busload, fifty or sixty, but after that our numbers steadied. In the few days after, we lost a few more, mostly those who'd been aligned with the instigators who now felt they no longer had a community and didn't know how to have the team be their community.

After that, if someone left, it was usually for other reasons—health, family, unfinished legal obligations that needed to be cleared up, and in a couple cases, simple frustration with having to be on the Can-Do Team. But by the sixth week, we had stabilized as a group, so any new absences were immediately apparent.

One morning, Dennis and Jack weren't at breakfast. We usually sat at the same table with them.

We asked Perf about it that afternoon. "Are people still being selected out?"

"No," he said. "Those of you who are still here, we expect you to complete."

"Then where are Dennis and Jack? And Wayne and Bruce? John and Lino?"

"They're jogging ahead."

"Excuse me?"

Perf said, "Have you noticed that when the group runs in the morning, some of you run ahead and some of you run behind, because everybody runs at their own pace. Some of the people who aren't here have jogged ahead."

"They're in different groups now? Different sessions?"

"They've jogged ahead," was all the answer he'd give us.

At the end of that session, however, Perf pulled José and me aside and handed us an appointment card. "Come see me right after dinner. You can skip tonight's session on Praxis geology. It's a recap on the scorch zone."

Dinner should have been hearty that evening. We'd been making good progress. We'd had a lot of sessions about fish-farming and aeroponics, so our tanks were filled with fattening salmon and our test gardens were starting to flourish. But instead of the expected feast, we were served soy-rations and vitamin water. Alec came in just long enough to say, "This is to remind you what life on Praxis will look like if you don't get the crops in. You had expectations. They weren't fulfilled. You're disappointed. You should be. Now you have another incentive. Because it's not just about surviving anymore—it's about succeeding beyond survival. It's about growth."

Point taken. Can do.

We met with Perfessor in his office. It wasn't more than a cubicle, but it was a cubicle large enough for three men and a coffee machine.

"Cappuccino?"

"Sí, gracias."

"Yes, please." I poked José. "We'd better enjoy this. I don't think there'll be cappuccino on Praxis."

Perf shook his head. "Not true. The first farm-udders are already producing. And there are several small test sites for coffee plantations that seem to be thriving. If they survive the weather, you'll have coffee. If not, you'll have to dedicate a factory. But you'll do that anyway if you want pineapples and bananas and starfruit."

"Really?"

Perf nodded. "Es verdad. There are a lot of things we haven't told you about Praxis—things you won't be told until you arrive."

"Why is that?"

"Well, part of it is that if we tried to tell you everything, your training and orientation would take eighteen months and it still wouldn't be complete. And the other part of it is that you'll learn it faster onsite—when your survival depends on it."

He looked at us both. "How do you feel you're doing? Are you keeping up? Falling behind? Getting ahead?"

"I think we're keeping up," I said.

"I agree," José added.

"Just keeping up?"

"Well—I hate to be judgmental—after all the communication trainings we've done, I mean, about not being arrogant and self-righteous, I'd feel like I was—"

"Just say it, James."

"I think we're doing better than some. If this were jogging, I'd say we're coming up on the forward group."

"You don't see yourself as leaders?"

"I think we're leaders in what we're good at. Some of the other guys look to us for direction sometimes."

"Maybe it was all our years as contract students—" laughed José. "Maybe we actually learned something after all."

"But there are a lot of other guys who know stuff too." I said. "More than us. So we follow their lead."

"Actually …" Perf said, "That's a kind of leadership too. Giving power away. Passing authority on to the most appropriate individual."

"I never thought of it that way."

"Of course not. Most people don't." Perf sipped slowly at his coffee. "Let me ask you something." He looked at both of us with that same penetrating expression he used in the training room. This was the point of the meeting. "How's the state of your marriage?"

"¿Perdón?"

Sometimes when José became anxious—or scared—he'd slip back into Spanish. I don't think he realized.

"How's your marriage?" Perf repeated. "Is it still a marriage of convenience? Or has it become a real partnership?"

I looked to José. We exchanged a glance. I wasn't sure how to answer the question and neither was he.

"I think—" I began carefully. "I think we work well together."

José agreed. "Sí. Es bien."

"So you'd call it a partnership?"

We looked at each other again. We hadn't talked about our marriage at all. Not since—that day.

"We haven't really … I think we're doing pretty good, I mean, I feel good about it, I haven't asked José, but I'd guess he feels the same way. I think this is one of those things that men don't talk about. Relationships, I mean. Marriage."

"Some men don't," said Perf. "You don't."

"I guess not."

"So?" Perf asked again. "If I was holding a gun to your head, how would you describe your marriage?" He grinned.

"I don't know—"

"Who do I have to ask to find out?"

"Uh—me, I guess. But I—"

"Make something up," he encouraged.

"Well, um. Yeah, we're pretty good together. Um—" I looked over at José. He was waiting for my answer too. "I feel like we're partners. No, it's more than that. I feel like we're friends. I feel—no, that's wrong. We're closer than that. We're … I guess you could call it family. We take care of each other."

"Sí. Familia. Es muy bien."

"Took you long enough to say it," said Perf. "What kind of family?" he asked. "Brothers? Or husbands? What's the relationship?"

"Uh—" I was about to say "husbands" but that would have been an automatic response. I understood what Perf was asking. What was our emotional investment in each other? It was one of those things we just never said. Maybe because we were afraid the answer might not be enough? Or maybe even more afraid that the answer would be more than we were willing to admit. Not just to each other, but to ourselves. Testing a relationship is like doing quality control in a hand-grenade factory.

Perf was still waiting for one of us to answer. "You don't know yet, do you?"

José and I looked at each other. Neither of us spoke.

"Right," said Perf. "Let me tell you something. Men don't know how to have relationships. Neither do women, but that's a different discussion, not relevant in this situation. The truth is—the evidence demonstrates it everywhere—most human beings do not know diddly-squat about how to treat each other, let alone love each other."

I looked at my hands, embarrassed. I looked back to Perf. I shrugged. "Yeah, you're right. But … that's the way we are."

He looked right back at me. *"But that's not the way you have to be!* That's the whole point of all those afternoon sessions. It's about teaching you all how to get along with each other like adults—like human beings who know they're riding the roller coaster of grief and joy and anger and triumph and fear and ecstasy— and are able to connect to others so they can share it. ¿Comprendes?"

"Sí."

"Yes, sir."

"So, look—I have an assignment for you." He sat back in his chair, it squeaked as he did so. He slurped at his coffee and considered his next words. "Intimacy."

"¿Perdón?"

"Intimacy," Perf repeated. "Intimacy. Find out what it is. Come back when you think you know."

"Huh? How—?"

"Figure it out, James. I will not discuss strategy. You know that."

"But … can I ask *why*—?"

"Why? Praxis, that's why."

Fifteen

We walked out into the gardens. The night-blooming flowers had already opened and the air smelled of sweetness and sprinklers and freshly mowed grass. I took José by the hand and led him to a stone bench. We sat facing each other, straddling it between us.

"Nice night," he said.

"Yeah."

"Romantic, kinda."

"Yeah. If we were boyfriends, it would be perfect."

"We're not boyfriends, we're husbands."

He laughed. "Yeah. We're just like any other married couple—we live together and we don't have sex."

That joke was so old it was in a wheelchair. But it could still get up and dance. It was only funny because it was still true.

Neither of us said anything for a moment. Finally, I nodded back toward the offices. "Do you understand what all that was about?" I asked.

"I think it was about us not having sex."

"Yeah, that's what I thought too."

"Do you want to?"

I shook my head. "I dunno. You?" That was the safe answer.

He shrugged. "I think Perf was testing us for something?"

"What?"

"Maybe … I'm just guessing here … but maybe he wants to see if we're jogging ahead."

"No." I dismissed the possibility. "We still have nine weeks to go. Sometimes I think we're barely keeping up."

"He sees the larger picture. And I think we're doing better than just keeping up." José reached over and tapped my hand. "I think Señor Perfessor wants us to conduct a personal inquiry, not a theoretical one. He wants us to have a conversation about ourselves. Because, I think … he wants us to be husbands. Real husbands."

"I always—" I took a breath. "The way I was raised, marriage was about love. Hugging, kissing, fucking your brains out, making babies, raising them, getting old together until you can't stand each other anymore, all that stuff. But … the legal definition only says two or more people in a committed partnership with specific goals and responsibilities. I'm not sure that says marriage as much as it says corporation. And that brings us back to the assignment, because that's not intimacy."

José sighed. He didn't know either. "What do you think intimacy is?"

I hesitated. I took a breath. I spoke carefully. "Growing up, I thought intimacy meant all the physical stuff that you're not supposed to know about until you're old enough, but when you're old enough you're supposed to know that it also means some kind of emotional connection—something special. But nobody tells you that. You're supposed to know it already. It's just …" I shrugged. "I don't know."

"Openness," said José, abruptly. "Vulnerability. Honesty. Like we keep talking about in the trainings."

"Okay," I said. I wasn't sure where he was going.

"Here's what I think," José said. "I think intimacy is what happens when two people stop being afraid of each other and start trusting each other. No—" He shook his head. "That's not right. Let me try it another way. You know how when you're in the shower with all the other guys, you know how you're not supposed to check them out, but you do it anyway, when no one's looking? And you worry they're checking you out—like everybody's comparing?"

"I don't do that," I said. "I go kinda blank, like I'm not there."

"Yeah, that's part of what I'm getting at. You withdraw inside of yourself so you don't have to be there," José agreed. "I've seen you do it. I try to say something to you—about anything—and you just grunt. You don't want to be social with no clothes on. Like it's uncomfortable for you."

"Yeah, it is," I admitted.

"So now we know what the opposite of intimacy is."

"Being shut down?"

"Yeah. And the opposite of that is trust."

"So intimacy is trust?"

"I think that's part of it." José hesitated. "Do you trust me?"

"I wouldn't have married you if I didn't."

"No, I mean—really trust?"

"I don't know—I mean, I don't know what you're asking."

"Okay, so look—let's go back to the showers. Do you talk to me in the shower? If you really trust someone, you're not afraid to be naked in front of them. You can look at him, he can look at you. It's no big deal. And you can talk about stuff—even to the point where you're so interested in what you're talking about, you forget you're naked."

"So intimacy is about getting naked?"

"I think being naked is part of it. I think."

"You've been there? You've done that?"

"Yeah."

"With a guy?"

"No. With a girl. It was good. It was wonderful. We just sat naked and talked for hours. About everything."

"I don't think men do that. I don't."

"I think that's the point." José said, "I think that's what Perf wanted us to notice. "We're not intimate." Then he asked. "Have you ever been intimate? With anyone? With a girl?"

"I've been with girls."

"Have you been *intimate*? Like we just defined it?"

"Like *you* just defined it."

"So the answer is no."

I shrugged. He was right. "Okay, why didn't you stay with your girl?"

"I wanted to. She's the reason I didn't go back to Buenos Aires. But she wanted a career more than she wanted me." He took a beat. "I'm over it. Pretty much. Maybe I was lucky to find out so quickly."

I didn't know what to say to that, so I didn't say anything.

José frowned. "You've never been that kind of intimate with anyone, have you?"

"I'm a dork, remember? No social skills."

"Even dorks can fall in love."

"Yeah, well—" I glanced over at him. "That's part of the reason why I chose Praxis. So I wouldn't have to—" I stopped because it was hard to finish the sentence. Another breath. One more try. "So I wouldn't have to have—a relationship. I'd have a good reason why not, okay?"

"I'm sorry," José said.

"For what? It's not your fault."

"I'm sorry for pushing you into this conversation."

"It's okay," I said.

"I think …"

"What?"

"I think I just figured something else out. About intimacy."

"I thought it was about being naked."

"It's about being emotionally naked. Physically naked just helps getting there. It's about being so open and so vulnerable that you can say anything and feel safe that your partner isn't going to judge you. And you can listen to anything he says and you don't judge either. You just understand why he feels that way. And it makes you closer."

"Yeah," I said. "That sounds good on paper."

"James. This conversation—this is an intimate conversation. Isn't it?"

"We're not naked though—" I said it as a joke.

"You want to get naked?" José started unbuttoning his shirt.

"No—it's all right." I put out a hand to stop him. "Not necessary."

He stopped and looked at me. "So there's a limit to your intimacy? You'll talk about stuff, but only until it's time to get really naked?"

"Please don't psychoanalyze me—"

"I'm not. I'm doing communication analysis."

"Same thing."

Abruptly, José demanded, "James. Why did you marry me?"

"It seemed like a good idea at the time—"

"An honest answer, James."

"I didn't think—" I shut up. "It wasn't—oh, never mind."

"Say it!" José demanded. "That thing."

"Nothing—"

"Nothing hell! What were you going to say?"

I took a deep breath. "We didn't get married to be lovers. We got married to go to Praxis."

José looked hurt. Or disappointed.

"Wasn't that what you wanted?" I asked.

"Of course—" He stopped.

"Okay, what? Your turn."

"I didn't—" He took a breath and recomposed himself. He began slowly. "I knew you were het. I knew who I was marrying. And if it would get me to Praxis—get us both to Praxis—that was fine with me. But y'know something funny? I actually like you. In spite of yourself. You're interesting. Sometimes you're even funny. And you're smart. And even though you don't see it, you're thoughtful. You watch out for me—that means something.

He paused. His voice became softer. "About a week ago, when a bunch of the guys started laughing in the showers about daisy-chaining and sandwiching each other, I started thinking. I mean, really thinking … and I realized that if you ever came to me and said you thought we should rechannel, I wouldn't say no. But we've never talked about it and I think that's what we're supposed to be doing now. I think that's the conversation Perf wants us to have." José studied my expression, suddenly realizing. "But that didn't even occur to you, did it?"

"José," I said, pulling my hand away. "I gave up on sex a long time ago."

"Nobody does that." And then he realized and his expression changed, almost to one of horror.

"I did. I had it turned off!" I didn't realize how angry I was until I said it. But I wasn't angry about the sex—or the lack of it. I was angry about being pushed into admitting it. "I got tired of being ignored. Politely rejected. Or given that look. And yeah, there were places where you could go … to be used and forgotten. I got tired of those too. I believed that there was something more because it looked like everybody else was having it, but not me. I was like a Christmas orphan with his nose pressed to the window wondering why everybody else was laughing and celebrating and having a wonderful time and I wasn't—so one day I figured out that I was making myself unhappy wanting something I was never going to have. So I went and had it turned off. And yeah, maybe I should have told you before this, maybe I should have told that interviewer too, but I figured if we're going to a planet that's all men, I'll finally be in a place where it won't matter if I don't—if I don't. Okay?"

José reached over and took my hands in his. "It's all right, James. I get it. And you're fine with me. You really are." He wouldn't let me pull my hands away. "James, you don't get it, do you? You're a hero to me. You always have been. You're so smart and so capable and so dependable—you don't see how good you are, what a strength you are, do you?"

I shrugged. "I can be capable."

"You're more than that. But you don't let yourself realize it. And that's okay. Because I do. And I'm glad we're married. And like I said before, everybody defines marriage for themselves in their own way. So this is ours. And I can be happy—satisfied with it if you can."

"Okay." I thought about what he was saying. "Um. José?"

"Yeah."

"Rechanneling? Is that something you want to do? Because ..." I swallowed hard. "I don't know if I can do that, but if it's important to you, I mean, if it's really that important, we can—talk about it, I guess."

He patted my hands and let go. "Thank you. I get it—that it's a big thing for you to say. And I'm glad you said it. That means a lot. But...that's not something we have to decide tonight. Not for a while. We have to figure out how to be husbands before we can be lovers."

"Okay." I felt relieved.

We went back to our cubicle then. The evening session was still going on, so we were alone in the showers. "José?" I asked.

"¿Sí?"

"Do you want me to scrub your back?"

"That would be nice, thank you."

After a while, he told me to turn around and he scrubbed my back. That was nice. It didn't mean anything more than that, but it was nice.

sixteen

The next day, at the start of the afternoon session, Perf asked us if we wanted to share anything with the rest of the group. José stood up, but Perf waved him back down. "I think James should be the one to speak."

I stood up.

Almost immediately, Perf waved me back down. "Thank you, James. That was all I needed to know."

The whole room laughed, but almost immediately the laughter turned into applause.

Perf waved me up again. "No, keep standing, James."

I did.

"Do you understand what just happened?"

"Yes." I looked around. "I don't share."

"And why is that?"

"I don't share."

"And why is that?"

"Because—I don't."

"Yes, we got that part."

"Because—I didn't think that what I had to share was important enough to bother anyone else with."

"Really? Go on."

"Everybody else has shared a lot of deep stuff. I'm not that deep."

When the laughter stopped, I said. "Well, I don't think I am."

"And the truth is?"

"The truth is that there's a lot going on inside of me and I don't—I don't want to talk about it."

"But you did talk about it last night. With your husband."

"With José, yes."

"With your husband."

"With my husband."

"You don't use that word much, do you?"

"No, I don't."

"Because—?"

"Because …" I looked down at José, sitting next to me. "Because I thought—I thought it was just a way to get to Praxis. A marriage of convenience."

"When you got married?"

"Yes."

"And now…?"

"Now, I don't know—" I stopped. "I mean, I do know. I just don't know how to say it. José is—well, he's just the best friend I've ever had. Maybe the only friend I've ever had. I wouldn't ever do anything to hurt him. And I know it's selfish to say this, but I can't risk losing him. I don't want to be alone again. So, um, yeah—he's my husband."

That's when I felt a hand grab mine. I glanced down to see José smiling up at me. He squeezed my hand, an avalanche of meaning and emotion.

Later, after lunch, but before we returned to the

training room, I took José aside. "I want to tell you something."

He gave me the I'm-Listening look.

"If it's something you want, something you need, if it's something we need to do to be … I guess, complete, then okay, I'll do it. For you."

"No," he said. "If you do it, you'll do it for us. Only for us. It has to be for you too."

"Yeah, okay. Yes."

We hugged. And this time, I kissed him. It was nice. A little strange. But nice.

I wasn't ready to be turned on again. But … maybe nobody is ever ready for anything.

seventeen

We had prime rib for dinner. An acknowledgment. We were succeeding as a team. As a community.

And then—halfway through dessert, it was over.

Perf came into the dining room and said, "As soon as you finish dinner, grab your stuff and get to the buses. We've got a portal train leaving tomorrow night and not a lot of time to load it."

"Huh? What? We weren't supposed to go for another six weeks."

"Yeah, well, schedules change. There was a sudden opening and we grabbed it. We have room for you, if you're ready." He looked around the room. "Are you ready?"

We all looked at each other. Suddenly, the trip to Praxis wasn't a hypothetical anymore. It was real.

I felt a sudden wash of uncertainty, fear. José grabbed my hand and said, "We made it. This is it!"

A murmur of whispers spread across the room as various others checked with their friends, their partners, their husbands.

I took a breath. I bent to José, "Whither thou goest…?"

He stood up. I stood up with him. "We're ready." And then behind us, two others stood up. "Let's go." And on the other side of the room. "We're ready." And a few more, "Let's roll." And then the applause started, and the cheering.

Perf held up his hands for silence and the room quieted down. "All right," he said. He checked his watch. "We've got 45 minutes until the buses pull out. If you're not there, you're not going. So this is your last chance to bail." And then he added, "Good luck. You're going to need it. Don't screw it up. That'll reflect badly on me. On us."

He started to turn away, then remembered. "Oh, one more thing. Alec asked to go with you. I approved. For some reason he thinks you're not assholes anymore, only possibilities. All right, go. We're on a deadline. Run."

None of us had much to grab. We'd packed our go-bags a week ago. Another exercise, we thought at the time. Now, we knew.

We started boarding the buses only fifteen minutes later. The band members were the last to board. They formed up and played an old one called "Goodbye." Tyler sang the vocal. He had a surprisingly good voice.

When the last bus was filled, we rolled out. Only Randy and Richard didn't board. Randy had a breakdown and Richard stayed behind with him. Whether or not they'd come later on, or even be allowed to, nobody knew, not even Alec.

We rode all night. Most of us tried to sleep on the bus. I couldn't. I stayed awake, José snoring softly on my shoulder, and wondered and worried and just felt weird.

We'd been taught meditation exercises, but I couldn't get into it. We'd been told that worrying doesn't work; it doesn't produce any useful result. But the mind doesn't work that way. It needs some kind of completion. And I wasn't complete.

Because José and I weren't complete.

I must have fallen asleep, because I came awake with my arm around him. And maybe that was the answer.

Gray light blurred sideways through the grime-streaked windows of the bus. The horizon was a distant glare. And we were rolling to a stop. Ahead was a tall, barbed wire fence, meters high and apparently meters thick as well. We had to roll slowly through a formidable-looking set of scanning frames, then forward again for another kilometer or two, past what could have been bunkers or some kind of weapon emplacements, and then through another scanning gate. And a few klicks more, a third one.

Eventually, the buses rolled down into a staging area and we poured out and lined up. We were tired, bleary-eyed, and disheveled—also excited, anxious, and uncertain.

The monitors were waiting for us. They ushered us into an antiseptic white facility and had us put everything we intended to take with us onto a conveyor belt. All that stuff had to go through a rigorous inspection and decontamination.

Then they had us strip naked and discard our clothes from the training camp so we could go through our own prep. Eventually, after six kinds of scanning they pointed us toward the showers for a good scrubbing. We were told to raise our arms and turn around repeatedly while we were sprayed and foamed and jetted and foamed and sprayed three more times.

José and I looked at each other and began laughing. He looked around. I looked around. Then we started laughing even more. That got us some strange looks from those nearby and that just made us laugh even more. José said, "It's okay. I'll explain later." Several smiled and waved.

Finally we were hot-air blasted until we were dry. We filed out feeling better, we got scanned a few more times, and finally exited into a dressing room where we were given lightweight jumpsuits to wear. "I'm surprised they didn't shave our heads," said José, pulling his pants legs up.

"And everything else," I joked.

One of the monitors overheard us. He said, "We used to. But not anymore. It's not as necessary as we originally thought. Have a safe trip."

After we passed through another set of gates where our handprints and footprints and eyes were scanned, after our embedded chips and tattooed bar codes were checked, we regrouped in the mess hall, a room large enough to hold all one hundred and sixty-seven of us who made it through the training. Several familiar faces rejoined us. They didn't say much about where they'd been, just some specialized instructions appropriate to their skill sets.

Meanwhile, breakfast was an unprecedented feast— everything we were leaving behind. All kinds of cereals and fruits and juices. Apples, peaches, apricots, oranges, tangerines, pineapples, more. Orange juice, peach nectar, tomato juice, apple juice, cranberry juice. A huge rack of tea and seasonings. A variety of breads, sweet rolls, buns, bagels, even cake. Cheeses, more cheeses than I had ever seen. Trays and trays of different meats, bacon, ham, hash, chicken, turkey, even pork and beef roasts with a carving chef behind them. A lot of fish, smoked salmon, shrimp, whitefish, sardines, kippers, more. And vegetables—all kinds of potatoes, of course, carrots, mushrooms, green beans, asparagus, corn. An amazing salad bar—and beyond that a dessert bar that defied imagination.

Oh, and coffee. Lots of it.

We were told to take our time and eat as much as we want. We didn't have to be told that twice. We joked, "And the condemned men ate a hearty meal." Ha ha. And you notta gonna like Wednesday either.

Breakfast was at least ninety minutes. We had seconds, we had thirds. This was the last time we'd ever have some of these things. We made the most of it.

Afterward, we regrouped in another seminar hall. Markham strode in and welcomed us. "There's not a lot to say that hasn't already been said, and I know you're impatient to board the train. And we want to get all of you aboard and checked in as quickly as we can. It's going to be a little cramped, thirty of you to a car, but you'll each have your own private cabins. The assignments are posted outside, and you can pick up your belongings there too.

"I can't tell you how long the trip will be, they're still routing. The quickest we've ever had a transport go through was seven days, the longest was five weeks. That wasn't fun for anyone. But we think we can get you to Praxis in two weeks, maybe less. Make the best use of the time that you can. There are a lot of instructional courses to download. There will be daily check-in seminars and exercises, you'll get a schedule. There will be a gym in each of the cars. Keep yourselves in shape. Use the treadmills to do your daily running. Take long showers; that's not a problem, the water gets recycled. And while the food won't be as good as it was this morning, you won't starve to death either. You've been well trained. But it'll be a long trip, so don't get lazy. Don't get sloppy. Don't lose your edge. Congratulations, you're on your way."

The train was impressive on the outside—a chain of huge pill-shaped cars, each one as wide as five ordinary train cars. They had to be wide to hold all the supplies and the massive equipment the colony would need— and the cars needed to be large because there was a limit on how long a train could be, so each car needed to be its own self-sufficient environment, as the whole train was going to pass through multiple hostile environments, low-gravity, high-gravity, low-pressure, high pressure, possible storms, probable vacuum, and a few below-ground tunnels so the contents—us—wouldn't get roasted by heat or radiation.

And finally, we boarded.

José and I found our cabin easily. We closed the door behind us, looked at each other, and after a long uncertain moment, we started laughing again. "We've come a long way."

"And we still have a long way to go."

I pulled down the bed so we could sit side by side. I put my arm around his shoulders and pulled him close. I looked at us in the mirror opposite, met his gaze and said, "Thank you."

"For…?"
"For everything."
"Uh-huh, yes," he agreed. "Everything."
We were on our way.

ABOUT THE AUTHOR

David Gerrold's work is famous around the world. His novels and stories have been translated into more than a dozen languages. His TV scripts are estimated to have been seen by more than a billion viewers.

Gerrold's prolific output includes stage shows, teleplays, film scripts, educational films, computer software, comic books, more than 50 novels and anthologies, and hundreds of articles, columns, and short stories.

He has worked on a dozen different TV series, including *Star Trek, Land of the Lost, Twilight Zone, Star Trek: The Next Generation, Babylon 5,* and *Sliders.* He is the author of *Star Trek*'s most popular episode "The Trouble With Tribbles."

Many of his novels are classics of the science fiction genre, including *The Man Who Folded Himself,* the ultimate time travel story, and *When HARLIE Was One,* considered one of the most thoughtful tales of artificial intelligence ever written. His stunning novels on ecological invasion, *A Matter For Men, A Day For Damnation, A Rage For Revenge,* and *A Season For Slaughter,* have all been best-sellers with a devoted fan following. His young adult series, *The Dingilliad*, traces the healing journey of a troubled family from Earth to a far-flung colony on another world. His *Star Wolf* series of novels about the psychological nature of interstellar war are in development as a television series.

A ten-time Hugo and Nebula award nominee, David Gerrold is also a recipient of the Skylark Award for Excellence in Imaginative Fiction, the Bram Stoker Award for Superior Achievement in Horror, and the Forrest J. Ackerman lifetime achievement award.

In 1995, Gerrold shared the adventure of how he adopted his son in *The Martian Child*, a semi-autobiographical tale of a science fiction writer who adopts a little boy, only to discover he might be a Martian. *The Martian Child* won the science fiction triple crown: the Hugo, the Nebula, and the Locus. It was the basis for the 2007 film *Martian Child* starring John Cusack and Amanda Peet.

Gerrold's greatest writing strengths are generally acknowledged to be his readable prose, his easy wit, his facility with action, the accuracy of his science, and the passions of his characters. An accomplished lecturer and world traveler, he has made appearances all over the United States, England, Europe, Canada, Australia, and New Zealand. His easy-going manner and disarming humor have made him a perennial favorite with audiences.

David Gerrold is the 2022 winner of the Robert A. Heinlein Award.